CALL IT A DIFFICULT NIGHT

Call it a difficult night

Mishka Hoosen

ISBN: 978-0-9870282-6-6
ebook ISBN: 978-1-928476-22-1

Deep South
contact@deepsouth.co.za
www.deepsouth.co.za

Distributed in South Africa by
University of KwaZulu-Natal Press
www.ukznpress.co.za

Distributed worldwide by
African Books Collective
PO Box 721, Oxford, OX1 9EN, UK
www.africanbookscollective.com/publishers/deep-south

NATIONAL ARTS COUNCIL
OF SOUTH AFRICA

Deep South acknowledges the financial assistance of
the National Arts Council for the production of this book

Cover design: Liz Gowans and Robert Berold
Text design and layout: Liz Gowans
Cover background: Manuscript letter by Emma Hauck (1878 - 1920)
"Herzensschatzi komm" [Brief an den Ehemann]
"Sweetheart come" [Letter to her husband], 1909, Inv. No. 3622/4
© University Hospital Heidelberg, Prinzhorn Collection

For all of them, for all my loves

⌘

No-one else sees him, but he's come from that other place now, made himself from shadow to stand there. Lean, blonde, ragged, he stands in the corner holding a bull's skull to his face. There are beads hung around his neck, and long scars down his arms. He speaks in a rough murmur all through the night. Some part of me, a dream-voice in my gut, says he is my brother. My brother but something else, something closer. Close as a son. And the horns of the skull grow larger and tangled like antlers until it is a stag's skull. The empty eye sockets and his eyes he hides in their shadow are howling. He calls me to the spirit world. You draw a line in the dust and you cross it, into that other place. The voices come from there. I ask him why. He says because I must go there. There's no more cheating that debt, he says. Things come back. Things echo. You had a good long run of it, on fire like you were. On the run all the time. Now you come back. You come back through fire.

The first time I heard him was just before my final breakdown, a few months into my first year of university. Slowly, like a flame catching, my mind and nerves lit and ran rampant. Ideas grew larger than me, than my entire existence. Monstrous and bright, everything connected by song, by meaning, by fine, fine tendrils I mapped out in notecards and twine on my walls, above my bed. I would stay up night after night, trying to write fast enough to catch everything. No matter how small or prosaic, every action, gesture, object, became prophetic. Everything that had ever existed echoed against each other, reflected and connected in bright ringing patterns till I cried, awed by the endless symmetry of the world, the elegance of the puzzle I was set to solve. I was a detective following leads and patterns, suspicions and stories to find the inmost secret of the world, the luminous key that would open all the doors, redeem all the suffering, save and grace and shatter me.

It consumed me, opened up thousands of doors of reasoning, countless reflections and epiphanies that in the waking world showed themselves to be absurd. Sometimes worse than absurd. Every idea and theory could turn on me in an instant, and they did. One minute I'd be overcome with the elegance of an idea, the delicacy and strength of a connection I'd found, and the next, like an ambigram, it would turn on itself and show me its darkness, its foreboding. I stared and muttered for hours in front of my mirror, convinced that in that other room, behind it, there was another me, whole and lovely, untouched and always young, always laughing. But no matter how I threw myself at the door, examined every inch of it, attempted to find the golden code that would finally let me in, nothing changed except the voices. In the shadows and corners of the room the air gathered itself like transparent cloth, congealed and moved till it formed a dog, a hare, a monster, a child. Each one whispered in a language I was obsessed with understanding. The more charged with destiny things became, the more I became filled with a holy dread. I found myself following leads and lines of thought and connection, more like a fugitive now than an explorer. Every book, every bit of dust, every shadow and flicker became a doorway I could duck into, a corridor filled with new monsters, and I had to believe that somewhere there would be an end to it, a coming out into light and leaf shadow and running water.

I drank myself to sleep, in secret. It was the only time I was unconscious. As soon as I opened my eyes everything burned itself into me. I heard voices where no one was speaking. I could see people's thoughts as fine tentacles, trailing behind them. The lines between things became visible, copper wires stitching the world into a mess of threads, a trap ready to spring.

One day in the university library I dropped a pile of books and threw myself through the revolving doors, ran to get away from all those whispers, the electric hum coming through the books, the staring eyes that I believed saw through me, saw my cowardly heart, my inadequate mind.

There was a shadow darting in the corner of my eye as I ran home. Like a cat one minute and a rabbit the next. I thought, with these things you have to stand still and quiet and they will come to you. And so I stood still and trembling and it came near me. It was a little girl, about nine years old. Dark hair and pale dress, brown arms and legs. She whispered that she had come a long way to see me, that she had things to explain. She whimpered that she was lost. I couldn't look at her directly, I was too afraid, but said to her that she could come home with me, that I would take care of her. She followed by my side, up the hill to my house, darting across the street and back again, I shouted at her to stay with me. "Those people can't see you, child. Walk with me or they'll run into you!"

People stared at me shouting at what they saw as empty air. Walking down the street I gathered dandelions from the pavement, wove them into a crown for her. When I tried to put it on her head, it fell to the ground, and she laughed at me for thinking she could come all the way into my world. "You're half here and half not, but I can only look through to your world. Come here." I shook my head, asked how I could ever do that, and why should I. "You want to lay down and sleep, don't you?" she asked. I said nothing and walked home, opened the gate for her to pass.

When we got inside she perched on a stool at the kitchen table, and I turned to pour a saucer of honey to give her. I'd heard somewhere honey was the food of other worlds as well. The sun streamed over the wood and pooled in front of her, leaf shadow moving over her. It was hard keeping her in focus. She moved under the skin of things.

When I turned to put the saucer on the table in front of her, her eyes were gone. Where her green eyes had been there were two dark holes, ringed with scar tissue. Her mouth was moving without making a sound, but I understood every word. It came through the afternoon light between us and entered my mind through my mouth. She called me a murderer, said that I had killed someone's name, someone I loved dearly. She wouldn't say who. I thought, why a name? Why not the person outright? And she said, "What do you think is worse? Which death? You know how many there are. Which death is the final one?" The bile rose and burned in my throat.

Her small mouth pulled into a sneer as she mocked me, called me a coward and a murderer. I shouted at her to leave, called her a liar. Threatened her. Finally half-sobbed that she had betrayed me. *I let you into my house, you liar. You little lying monster.* She smiled. I grabbed the saucer and hurled it at her. It shattered on the wall, and she was gone. Instead, where the shards caught the light there was a trapline, tangled, and a small thing was tearing itself to pieces in it, screaming. I knelt and sobbed and pulled at it, muttering, "I'm sorry, I'm sorry."

Liz and James got home to find me muttering, "I'm sorry, I'm sorry for breaking the plate."

I swept up the shards as best I could, stared away from them at the floor and the corners, when they asked if I was alright. "I have to work. I have to get to my work."

When I came to myself again I was lying on the couch, long scratches on my hands, and someone calling, far off, for someone to hold me. For three days I lay on that couch delirious. The two worlds shone one over the other like panes of glass. When they shifted it caused me excruciating pain, running down my neck and into the side of my ribs. There was a grip on my throat and I tasted dried blood in my gullet. I couldn't eat or sleep. Someone brought me water and held it to my lips. All through the fever he stood there, my brother. Somewhere I was raking a knife down my arms, and a hare was screaming. For a moment I was a dog and held a hare in my teeth, its claws raking vainly at my jaw, the blood like a knife resting on my tongue. And I sobbed, "My boy, my boy."

My hands seized again and again. I heard talking from Liz, Lyra, James. I heard them murmuring to each other, taking turns to hold me. Keep me in this world. There was no rest for any of us. Each time I tried to cross the line and stand with him they would call me back. Ask me again and again where I was. His voice ran under everything, calling me, berating me for delaying, for being a coward. I begged on both sides. I asked to be left in one or the other of the worlds. I begged. My breath came shallow and my hands and throat were shot through with electricity. It came in waves. It pulled at me till I was ragged. Each time the current went through me, my spine felt as if it would snap. Every nerve stretched and raw. I begged. There was no pride left. I begged. *Let me go. Let me go to him. Please I am so tired. Please let me go. I am so tired. Where was God? Let me go home. Let me go home. Let the blood run out.* There was a roaring in my lungs. I sobbed like a child. Where do you go in your mind and where is there any rest? The walls shifted, and he stood there in the corner with a knife and called from the other world. Called through and with the fever. I heard someone say into a phone, "Come. She's not in this world."

Everything cut from its ties to the world and ran rampant. My lungs felt fit to tear. I was a dog with a hare in its teeth. I was trying to snap the neck, but it twisted in my mouth and I lost my grip again and again. It screamed against my tongue. I was a small child with a rabbit in its arms. My hands were too weak to snap its neck. The small heart beat hard against the ragged fur and my hands. The pupils open fit to swallow me. There was screaming in my lungs and in my ears and under my eyelids. Nothing left whole. Beset. Here are the many hands and claws at my nerves. Here are the voices screaming for me, ghosts come for my blood, to tangle in my hair. And they are calling to me as he calls, begging for my life.

⌘

Days later, I was transferred to the psychiatric hospital an hour away. I stuck my tongue out at the security cameras in the reception. I was taken to an examining room, weighed and measured. What've you been seeing? "Heaven and hell fighting it out in my living room. And I tried to kill myself in the garden under the quince tree. They say that was the fruit in the garden of Eden. Made sense, right? It was raining, and there were spirits calling through it. My brother especially. He keeps calling. He never stops."

The nurse on duty pauses. "You don't have a brother though."

"Not that anyone knows of."

"We're going to give you something to eat and let you see the doctor, okay?"

"Righto. Carl, right?"

I'm given a plate in the nearly-empty dining room, observed, as the entire corridor is, by the nurses' station. A cubicle firmly in the corner so no-one can sneak up on them, windows of glass with little round holes you can talk to them through. Dumb attempt at a Panopticon, I think, feeling smart for remembering stuff like this. There's only one old lady sitting at the next table, wearing leopard-print pyjamas and red nail polish on the toes of her remaining leg. She thanks the nurse who brings her medication, jerks her thumb at her retreating back, and mouths to me, "Give them hell." I nod solemnly. We're friends now. My dad approves, eating the stuff I won't touch, which is most of it. He's driven across the country and coast in a night and a day. He mutters, smiling, "Glad you made friends with Hopalong Cassidy." I spit my juice.

The doctor sees us after that. He seems nice. Old, solemn, but soft-eyed. Explains very patiently the consequences of what just happened. Because it's his identical twin brother who will see me later and be the downer of the two I can't remember exactly which of them told me. He points out scans that explain damage caused by these episodes. Later they'll define them as temporal lobe seizures. "If these continue at a frequent pace, you'd be either demented or brain dead by the time you're about 30 years old. But of course if we treat it well you won't fall into that delirium again." He looks at me. "So we need to control it."

He explains the synapses, how somewhere between one and another the message is scrambled, there is interference and the wrong signal is received. "Where does that interference come from?" He tells us they still don't know.

I hear that the Hmong tribes of northern Laos call this "the spirit catches you and you fall down." These are not the explanations any doctor ever agreed with.

I brought my own kind of totems into that place, around my neck. I tried to pronounce the songs the voices sang all night, but my mouth twisted and there wasn't enough breath left in my body to make a sound.

While I'm in a drugged haze, he points at scans and explains that tiny doorway, the briefest of gaps for the signal to pass through, how something has found that gap and is quicker than the original. I think to myself, *That's where the spirit comes in.* We talk about dopamine receptors and medication side effects while a shadow lopes in the corridor.

A year after that place, the water in the shower covers me with voices. I can't get away without slipping, and anyway they're still there. I stumble, claw at tiles. Try to scream but all that happens is my mouth twists. I am on my knees, counting tiles with prayers. After a little while, when the hot water is used up and the cold hits me awake, I get up. I dry myself on the floor. I get up and dress. I make an appointment with the one doctor left for me to trust.

She's a family friend, practically a blood relation. When I get into her office I ask about the baby, the new house.
"Right. Now we need to talk."
She sits up straight. Looks me in the eye. "Yes?"
"You remember those scans from the psych hospital last year?"
"Yes."
"Well what did they show?"
"They did show definite signs of epilepsy."
"And damage because of it?"
"... Yes."

I count crystal ornaments on her desk. I think I gave her one for her birthday once. I'm weighing up how much truth I've earned from her. I force myself to look up again. Her eyes are wide, her soft hands folded neatly on the desk, like a schoolgirl. She's wearing a brown headscarf that brings out her eyes.

Growing up, girls were told to cover their hair at dusk. "If you don't, the jinn will tangle in your hair and drive you mad."

"He said frequent damage would leave me…"

"Demented or brain dead or in a constant delirious state, yes I think I told you once –"

"I know you did. Now I want you to be honest with me, like no-one else has ever been. I'm begging you to at least give me that dignity, okay? Don't spare anyone or anything. Now, what would 'frequent' be?"

"… Once every two years would be considered frequent." She goes on, "How often do yours happen?"

"About once every two to three weeks, if I'm lucky. Sometimes more."

She's quiet. I breathe hard, stare into the corner.

Fuck. I say, "I told Eva once that I feel it, deep in me, that I won't be able to make it through another two of those intense seizures. That three-day ordeal. Maybe I could make it through one. I think I could just about survive one more, but not another. It would kill me, one way or another. Admit that you know, everyone knows deep down what they have left, how much more they can sustain. Now tell me, truthfully, is there physical evidence of this, or am I being a coward?"

She hesitates one second then says, "Yes. There is."

I swallow, I blink exactly once. I lean back in the chair. Put my hands behind my head. Cavalier. If you fucking cry you'll never stop. "Well, fuck. Guess I'd better book that skydiving trip soon then. Maybe get on a yacht and sail to Cuba too."

She smiles, half-hearted. "Let's talk about something else."

The outdoor recreation area

When they bring you in you learn by way of cigarettes and long whimpering animal nights to paint the stars from memory on the bench by the fence with a garden on the other side. At no time do they allow you into that garden, so you pace along the fence of the 'outdoor recreation area,' a paved space of about twenty paces long and five paces wide. You've walked it enough, counting. On the nights before the 800mg take effect you speak wildly before it hits. You recite Eliot, Neruda, Lorca, Byron, Harrison, fucking Bob Dylan, anyone, anyone. You speak for the fractured things you meet: the girl who picks apart her food with the furtiveness of a bird, watches the middle distance and murmurs. She is fourteen, brought here still in her school uniform, slapped twice by a nurse. She's set off the fire alarm twice by following the instructions on the glass: "In case of emergency..."

She meets your eye from too far away, half-lidded, drugged to swaying, her small feet seeming to swim in those school shoes. And she knows. She knows how unfair it is, to be this tired. "What language am I speaking?"
"English."
"I need a different one."

"I can teach you French if you like, love."

She shakes her head. "But I'm not in France. I'm not in France."

She sways to where a nurse waits for her. Spends three hours in front of the TV on mute. And here you are walking those twenty paces again and again till your walk becomes a stumbling then a fall, seeking a language for everyone, hunting it down, keen-scented and weary.

⌘

When it gets to where the voices start to ripple the air, you take the medication willingly. You swallow it dry and blink it away.

On the phone Sonya says "How ironic – you used to fight them tooth and nail when they tried to give it to you."
"Yeah well I'm too old for that shit."
"Jesus. You're twenty-one."
"Sonya, seventeen was already too old for this."

At some point in the night your girlfriend glares at you, asks, "Did you take them?"
"Of course I fucking took them, I don't need a nurse."
"You know why I'm asking. How many did you take?"
"Enough."
"Fuck, just give me the bottle. Let me just keep it, and when you want some you can ask."
"Who do you think you are?"
"Not the addict."
"Fuck you. The doctors have been trying to get me to take this since I was twelve. I'm finally fucking taking them. There's no pleasing you people."
"I'm not one of them."
"Yes you are."

She gets upset at that. Sits down and cries a little, "You go somewhere, you're always looking at two places at once, and most of the time I don't think you pick this one to focus on. You don't pick the one I'm in."

"I'm here now, though. I'm here with you and I love you. I love you here."

"You're only ever half in this world. So you only ever half love me."

It takes everything in you not to scream at that. Instead you clench and unclench your fists, look away from her to the corner, ignoring the moving light and the whispers there, counting tiles in the floor, reciting a nursery rhyme. You turn to her again, shake your head slowly. *Don't. Don't. Ever again.*

She turns away from you, leaves the bottle on the bedside table. When she leaves the room you take another three pills.

Next day when you're supposed to go with her to pick up her sister Charlotte from the airport, you take another one, not wanting her to see you ill. You've lost track of them now, but the voices still gather in the corners and nip at your heels and there's something shrieking in your lungs that you will run away from in any way left to you.

So you take another two.

Within half an hour your coordination's shot and you have to use a cane to walk. You stagger to the car where you sit sweating and reciting the opening of *Lolita* because the music of it keeps your head from spinning too much.

About twenty minutes out of town you pull over, mumbling to the two of them "Don't look" as you stumble out of the car and as far into the bushes as you can before you fall and vomit. You know Charlotte gets squeamish. When you've collected yourself you get back to the car, wash your mouth with water from the windshield wipers. When you eventually get back to the house you collapse into a seizure that lasts hours.

As if to get back at you for trying to fight them, they come back, voices like water pulling at you. When you were about ten you almost drowned in a rip tide. You swam furiously against it, thinking that if you could only swim fast and hard enough, you could get out of it. When a life guard swam up to pull you back to shore you glared at him as he came near, shouting that you didn't need anyone. He pulled you back anyway, and you crept off alone to the ridges as your mother wept thanks. You sat among the dune grass clutching yourself and staring out at all that water that felt as if it had gone right through to your marrow. All night you were awake, listening to the sea, crying till your voice gave out to be in it again. As if only by going back to it would the remnants of it in your bones be made quiet.

"Let me go, love. Please let me go. There's – it's here – it's here inside – let me go under. Go – let go – here – it's here."
But even as you say it there's something dragging at your ribs, digging its nails in to stay in this world.

She holds you and calls you back, again and again, every time you try to close your eyes. You whimper like a child.
"Tired – let me go home. Let me sleep."
"No. No you stay with me. Do you love me?"

You stare at her, her big eyes, her hands. You manage to nod yes. You try to say it too, but the voices are furious in your head, roil and seethe, tearing everything you see in two, and then in four, and then in eight, till everything is shattered out of recognition. When your back stops arching and your hands stop seizing because your body is no longer physically capable of doing that much, you lie there and sink into sleep, because there is nowhere else to go.

When you wake up you find no part of your body unworn or whole. You try to get up but you fall back, again and again. Your head spins and your ribs feel bruised. You only manage to sit up, everything in you strung together only because you're clenching your teeth sobbing dry saying, *Not the fuck like this and not now.*

A friend comes in, dear God how is there such goodness there for you for the asking?

"How're you feeling?"

"Like I got the shit beaten out of me."

"You look it."

"Oh, you should see the other guy."

Quick huff of laughter, only half-believing.

Only triumph you can get.

⌘

One night there are things with thin voices clawing between all those levels of air. You take down the mirror, lean it against the wall. Kneel. Take out your cheap pocket knife, bought on a whim. You choose your forearm, because it is easily seen and marked but not ostentatious. A sign for those in the know. But what do they know? The question beats inside you, flinging around your skull. *What do I know that they will know too? What is the mystery, the unnamed thing gnawing?* You can't look it in the eye. You draw the blade across your arm again and again till you think it's deep enough. You light a match, hold the knife to it. Soot spreads along the bright blade and mars it. You push the hot blade between the parted ridges of skin. Blood steams. You bite your collar. You're surprised you don't have to bite down as hard as you expected. You think, *This is right. This must be right.*

At boarding school in Michigan we tried salvia. A Mexican hallucinogen used in shamanic trances with names like Seer's Sage and Ska Maria Pastoria, that appealed to us, seeming incantatory, potent as we needed. It was my first girlfriend's idea. Theo was always one for the picturesque. She ordered some of the dried leaves off the internet, along with a bong she called "Beautiful" and a silver Zippo engraved with dainty scrollwork, doing nothing in half-measures. Three years later I found the same Zippo design in Johannesburg and bought it out of sentimentality. Flicking it open and shut, I'd watch the blue and red sparks ending in nothing when the wick frayed useless.

We were at Bear Lake for the weekend, early February or so. Deep snow in the fields, and we walked across them to a small copse overlooking a broad, snowed-over field, unmarred and still. We settled into a snowbank, and she cradled the bong and the flame in her hands, blew it to life. She took a long drag and tilted her head back. I sat facing her, watching the blue veins of her neck and her hair starred with snow. She looked at me, grinned, and came over to straddle my lap. She held her mouth to mine, blew in the blue smoke. She laughed then, eyes

green and bright, and I said *yes*. She held the bong to my
lips and I drew it in deep. We lay back in the snow waiting
for things to happen. She said she saw purple birds, and
a ring of light protecting us, sweeping across the field.
I saw snow, and the copse, and her, not like they were
before but like I'd seen snow when I was little, a child
reaching in the dark for the flurry of snow no-one saw.
Something else came alive in them. It was as if the smoke
had thrown cloth over the invisible thing so we could see
it moving. It wasn't much different from how things had
come before, except now, for once, I could hear more
clearly. The language the voices spoke in was clearer.

We'd make fun of the whole thing later, "Fucking purple
birds. What even." But what happened then and what
I couldn't let go of afterwards was that the voices that
ran under everything came up clearer. As if a weak radio
signal in another language cleared and you found you
could make out words, and in a while, the rhythms of its
syntax. It was the first time I could look the thing in the
eye and name it for what it was. I kept looking for that
same calm place, the steadiness in facing the beast, and
years afterwards, in South Africa again, I spent an obscene
amount on a salvia tincture. I took it again and again after
coming back from the hospital, against everyone's wishes.
I figured if the medication they'd given me simply put

the voices behind glass, still incomprehensible, I might as well make my own medicine, and put myself to the task of learning the language I was hearing.

I've heard and read that in the Amazon basin the far more powerful drug ayahuasca is taken in order to induce a spiritual journey – an ordeal for the sake of wisdom and healing. The ayahuasca vine is cooked into a powerful brew and drunk by the ceremony participants as well as the curandero – the healer guiding and overseeing this journey. The curandero will sing, accompanied by a leaf rattle. These songs are known as icaros. They are meant to guide the spirit through the journey into the spirit world, and back. Often the language used, a mix of Quechua and Spanish, and sometimes simple sounds, has no discernible meaning to the outside observer, springing as it does from the impulse and the spirit of the vine speaking through the curandero.

For the three days and nights of the fever, that boy/man my brother and son sang to me and I couldn't understand him. The song pulled at me, rose into my throat where it stayed, burning and mute. I had to tell him no, that I wouldn't leave for that other world, that I would stay in this one. All through the first night in the hospital, he stood silent as someone else, shadowy and old, face flaring into light only now and then, sang another song for me to stay.

The ceremony is an ordeal, make no mistake about that. Participants are given a bucket to vomit into, and are instructed to wear loose, comfortable clothing, and to disclose any history of martial arts training, so as not to harm themselves or others in the paroxysms of the drug. Often, the more the participant vomits, the more evil is said to be expelled. Years ago, Kira Salak, a writer for National Geographic who had suffered from depression most of her life went seeking a cure in ayahuasca. After hours of struggle and searing visions, she found a small black snake in her vomit. She claims to be cured of that depression, killed as it was when she pulled a small girl out of a burning circle of demons.

For years I've been fascinated with it, with what it might do. I've gone looking for medicine everywhere.

Everyone I've spoken to about it has warned me about the danger of the drug, the extremity of it. I think sometimes that extremity is what the world fears most now. In Michigan I used to climb the tallest trees by the lakeshores as storms rolled in, transfixed in that small ordeal of wind and water, the invitation open for death, the edges always in sight.

When I was about fourteen, my parents found out I'd been cutting myself. My father took me aside and, far from being angry, said he understood. We were alike, he said. We both have this thing in us that goes looking for the edges, seeing how far we can go before it leaves a scar. He asked me not to, though. He asked me to stay.

Once, driving back from the beach at Port Alfred, playing truant from the hothouse of Grahamstown, we turned to watch the sun setting in a slurring of cloud and fire, horizon and water, red and gold and the smallest streaks of green staining the sky, straight down, as if the land ended there, and the sun was falling with the seawater that must also be falling off that edge.

"Imagine if that were the edge, the end of the world, right there," someone said.

I murmured, "It would be such a comfort."

Night Keening

The devil
comes in at seven.
He comes in you grab him. Oh
he's your waking fiend that old hand
on the shoulder, your old bastard
your funny man
your tricking carney with his bright teeth and the smooth
click of a lock or clockwork
in the garish oleander nights.

There is no etiquette.
This fight of flint and tooth, go out to meet him
grab him by his smooth throat,
grab his shirt collar fling him
fling him
fling him
to the ground.

Even if it means you must make peace with your always-
breaking heart
and your frantic throat.
So be it.
Live with him.
Let it come.

My room

My roommate is a one-legged eighty-year old woman who writes her memories in blue pen on the backs of Dunhill Courtleigh cigarette boxes. She threatens nurses with her crutch, wears leopard print and red nail polish. Says within five minutes "You ever need a smoke luvvie you ask Aunty Cee." She lost her leg when a drunk driver slammed into her red BMW. Red is her favourite colour, even now, without her red car, there are the Courtleigh boxes, with their gold paper, their luxurious red, their white backs on which she writes all our names.

Out of everyone I am the only one who sees her small and vulnerable as she is. I come into the room after lunch when she has a lie-down because that's when her leg drives her mad with pain. And when she cries quietly *Oh I buried my Maria in her wedding dress. She was only 19. All the neighbours said how could I do that how could I put her in the ground in a wedding dress am I mad but do they want me to go back to the quiet house with my baby's white dress hanging in the cupboard? Do they want that?*

Night before she leaves she offers me her wedding ring, says, "You're like my little Maria come back to me. The Lord sent you."

I say, "Ag no, Aunty Cee, you need to keep it." I give her one of my totems, a pendant with a swallow. She's always called me her little bird. She cries in my arms. She gives me a gold bangle and says "You fly away my little bird, you fly. And never be ashamed to cry, it's God's medicine."

I hold her and hold her and she's this tiny old woman who used to be a champion sprinter and she's crying so hard she shakes in my arms, drops her crutch and leans on me. God's medicine.

Aunty Cee would turn the radio right up on a gospel station that played old hymns I'd last heard in a church outside Atlanta. I can still see that old woman on her bed, the cut off stump of her right leg quivering with some invisible pain, as she closed her eyes and sang, hands moving through the air with every word. Decided. Sure.

If heaven's not my home,
Oh Lord what will I do.
The angels beckon me
through heaven's open door.
And I cannot feel at home in this world anymore.

⌘

When I was about five or six, I was lying with my mother on the bed around dusk. It started to rain, then snow in the room. *Mama,* I said, *look it's snowing.* My mother thought I was just imagining it – I'd always had an overactive imagination, everyone thought. But it was there, there was no denying it. No-one saw it, but the rain wet my hair and pajamas, and the snow melted on my hands. It blew in through the windows, touched no-one else when I reached for it in the dark.

The dining hall

A man in the corner holds the bible and a notebook close to his heart and speaks of frequencies and conversations he overhears in the air. Every morning you ask how he is, and he says, "Thankful. I'm thankful I survived last night. They haven't caught me yet." Every night he says his prayers and walks to his room straight-backed and ready for the death he says he knows is waiting in the ceiling above his bed.

One afternoon I sit with him and he explains software programming, the side-effects of the Seroquel: "You're fainting every morning because you're standing up too quickly. The Seroquel slows down the valves in your brain that regulate the blood flow. Don't get up too quickly." The DSM-IV: "See, the number of diagnoses has more than tripled since the manual came out in the 50's. The more they expand their definitions, the more drugs they can sell, the more money they all make. Look at it some time. See how many symptoms you've got, and how many diagnoses you qualify for. It's like a menu."

Then he explains how an assassin could come in through the roof, or trick the guards, shoot down on him from the ceiling above his bed, or shoot from the top of the roof, into him, standing in the courtyard.

I say, "Gabe, you're so brave."

He says, "No, no. I have my Achilles' heel."

"Don't forget he was the greatest warrior alive, Gabe. Don't you dare forget."

When his son visits he closes his eyes and sweeps the boy up, takes him in his arms, eyes closed, shoulders at last given rest from a burden.

When I tell them they're mad for forbidding me to talk to him, the nurses up my dose from 100mg to 800mg overnight. I manage to pace the fence twenty times (*here, you fuckers*) before I fall and they take me to the bed again.

When Carnia is taken to the room at the end of the corridor again, that room the patients never mention and the nurses use as a threat (Thrice for me, once almost got Ativan in the arm by force, but they never managed. Eventually they gave up on me.) I murmur to Gabe, not even realizing I'm speaking aloud, "She's such a little girl, Gabe."

"There are thousands of others like that."

"Yes, but here's *this one*."

Touched

One night the ash-blonde girl I loved with the starving eyes brought home the skin of a goat they had slaughtered at the farm where she worked. I helped her clean it, scraping away the last scraps of flesh and fat. The blades bright as the moon. The scent of blood and somewhere beyond it a smell of autumn and beyond that the scent of early fruit. I smelt of blood for a week.

Outside there was a beech tree and from it the pale-winged starlings flew down into a trough of water. She watched them with eyes like the birds'. We did not nor ever could fly down from the beech tree to the bright water, though I did try to drown myself, once.

It had been a young goat with a coat the colour of blackberries. On the underside of the skin we are so much redness and richness.

I heated the blade of a knife with a match and pressed it into my arm. Scent of autumn and later, much later, the new fruit after winter has turned us raw. On the underside of skin we are so much richness.

It is cruel that there are this many hours in a night.

Someone cried in my arms when they took me. She held me hard and her hair was brown and gleaming, smelling like her breath did, tired and cold. She said sometimes I think you must be some kind of angel.

They all repeat their questions. They drug you till your pacing by the fence becomes a stumbling then a fall. They watch you empty-eyed as something low and small and hurt moves in your throat when they hook you up to the machines, tell you to breathe like this and like this till it's there again, that horrifying half-dream and hunted heart beating desperate in your chest and they keep you there so long that even your proud heart thinks of begging. They take the wires off and say calmly that it worked. But they don't know it's broken already, the smooth clockwork thing that was supposed to keep you with them. You stand with your hands flat against glass, talking and talking, saying do you hear me, do you see me, do you.

They are many and we are small and ragged and bite. Still you're touched, as they say, the women motioning to the head, the hair, your hair's always tangled, you *touched* or something? Something rising in your throat as the woman you stole roses for is dragged down the corridor with her cries echoing down and across and between these walls and God there's no word for that sound, moan, wail, cry, scream, human, animal, no word, no answer for it none and let no-one say they can imagine it because no-one can and the nurses say *"Yes, doctor, we gave her the 5mg but she's so strong, doctor, so strong, but yes, yes it's alright we've tied her down so strong, doctor, you'd never believe it but yes we'll wait for you."* And who will wait for you, still such a stranger standing there, so deep-down touched with fire?

Long ago they might have said it was God we heard. Long ago they would have said we have seen that next place, the ghost world. What a long way, and now the glass. And then the skin. We are all such strangers to each other.

I cried for hours and howled for God to come down and explain, to show me the trick. See here how the woman cut in half emerges from the starry box whole and in a blue dress. See here how the disappeared man reappears with a flower in his hand. See here how the burned flower turns into a white bird. Here is the trick explained. Here is the puzzle and the problem elegant and whole. God did not say anything and I howled and called and searched but He did not come.

I've loved so many people, reached up to faces, eyes, hands. One night someone I loved asked what I see and know and feel in these breathless hours. I told her as I kissed her throat. I told her *My veins have turned to rivers.*

I am worn down by voices, names, places, songs. I am word to the bone and the blood. She said, you live as if your skin were peeled off. I say, it was. I can't tell you how but it was.

When you kiss someone you love, you know in every vein you are young and fearless and mortal. Life beating its quick way red and dear under the skin, every moment telling you it's leaving, no kiss enough to break it, no love or sex enough to take away this strangeness between you, how lonely you are in your skin, where you go in it.

I say half-things in these broken words. My voice breaks and I reach up to what I love, I reach to touch a face or lips, wordless. Love makes things too dear to talk about, every touch a hazard, the be-all and end-all of the world. And skin always between us, till you rip it off, apart, open, raw to the redness underneath. And still I cannot touch your life, explain. You *touched* or something? *Yes, yes. I was and am and will be.*

⌘

Gabe is in his mid to late thirties. Dark hair, neatly groomed. Soft brown eyes. He is always impeccably neat, clean shirt, sometimes a tie too. Clean hands. Careful ways about him, like a dutiful office worker. He always says grace before meals. He waits until everyone has their food before eating himself. He is gentlemanly in his ways, soft-spoken. No one seems to talk to him.

The first time we meet I overhear him telling the nurses he's afraid to go to his room. He's asking to sleep in High Care. Why the hell would anyone want that, I think to myself, but he's afraid to be alone. "I am explaining to you that I know that I will die tonight. I can hear it. I feel unsafe and would like some help." He is so calm, so methodical. He's patient, explaining the situation to the nurse on duty. I can't see her, but I see him standing calmly at the counter of the nurse's station, in his slippers, holding his bible to his chest. He has a habit of placing his hands carefully spread and flat on the surfaces of tables, as if holding them down, in place.

Later, while he sits at the dinner table, clutching his bible and writing in a notebook, shaking, I come up to him and say hi. He glances at me out of the corner of his eye. But his politeness wins out, he smiles at me, says hello.

"Hey, look sir. I won't claim to know what you're going through, but I just want you to know that it's ok – I hear things too, and neither of us is crazy."

He smiles, explains kindly, "No, you see the voices I hear are at certain frequencies, but they are real. *You* are probably ill, some kind of psychosis perhaps, but what I hear is real."

I'm quiet for a while, the smile still on my mouth. I look away, swallow, then turn to him again.

He explains gently about the conspiracy against him, the secret radio signals he picks up on, where he hears voices discussing how they will have him assassinated. He is eloquent, well-educated, kind. I can't follow the technical parts – the explanation of the radio signals, the intricate workings of the conspiracy, but I listen, and where I can I ask him to explain. When I grasp something particularly subtle, he smiles and says, "Yes! Yes! Precisely!"

"They never listen to me," he says, indicating the nurses. "It's natural that they should think I'm somehow ill – they simply can't grasp what's going on, but they never try to understand either." He's quiet then, looks at the table. I reach for words that might show I think he's brilliant, that I won't pass judgment on what's happening to him because for all I know he might be entirely right. The world feels wide around me and I can't lay claim to it, can't hold anything down, like he does with his hands flat on the table. I am tiny and inadequate, he is the wrongly committed and I'm the one who is rightfully here. "Well, I don't know what to say, sometimes, to comfort people, and I don't always understand – I can't quite follow. But I can say this: I respect you, sir."

And he smiles, sheepish, and says, "No, but thank you."

Aunty Cee comes by, as he walks off, says to me "That gentleman's never spoken to anyone for so long before. I haven't heard more than ten words out of him before. He's a real genius, though. You know that?"

I nod. She nods, decided.

"A real genius. And a good man."

"The best," I tell her.

⌘

One night when I was very small, about six – or was it about fourteen? The truth is my childhood is a blur to me – a dream pierced sometimes by memories like smears of paint, like slashes in canvas – we drove for a long time through the countryside. I can't remember where it was, only that we drove through the night, and that at a bend in the road of some silent one-street town there was a burnt-out house the adults whispered about and didn't want me to see.

They said "Remember that –."

"Yes, God, horrible."

I was a sweet-hearted but difficult child, I think. Sometimes I'm told I was a spoiled brat, other times an angel. Never what I really was. I know I lived as if my skin were peeled off. I was nervous. Quick to forgive and forget a hurt, but some scar always stayed, some raw place, and one wound I covered and guarded like a cornered animal. The world became rife with omens. I carried a map of hidden rivers and riptides in my mind, nothing safe for long, no rest anywhere.

That night I was dozing while the adults spoke, but woke when something small and sharp-toothed came in through the gap at the window. About the size of a small child, it crept close to me and sheltered behind me, though I hated it and wanted it gone. It whispered to me to keep it safe. I tried to argue with it, tell it to leave but the adults wouldn't have believed me. And by then I'd learnt not to talk to them or about them aloud.

The bench by the fence

Last night all the light turned against me, burned wherever it touched, screamed under my skin. A small animal made out of that light twisted in my chest, raking at my ribs, shrieking. My spine pulled taut, my hands curled into themselves. Somewhere in it I turned to find the moon full outside my window, a drop of milk. I watched it make its way across the sky till it left the window. I recited every prayer in every language I knew. I gripped my hair in my hands, raked my nails across my arms, saying *This this this is my own blood this blood is my own my own this is here and mine and real my own blood no voice in it but mine.*

And out of it, my blood starring the long pale scratches, something low and old came up from the ground, murmured low in the throat, loped near to me and lay down, breathing warm in the dark, smell of the rain-washed ground under the quince tree, saying nothing but lying still, deep-breathed, in the long night. Then deep sleep.

When I woke up I took my time, fell twice, but as the dizziness and the nausea cleared I held onto the walls and got into the shower, where the water hit me awake and wild with cold and sun breaking in through the small window.

Outside, I perched on the arm of the bench and leaned my head against the wood of the fence, the scent of the garden heady. After about a minute, Gabe came out, holding his bible. I'd never seen him come out before during the day, without prompting.

"Hey Gabe."

"Hey," and he smiles, slowly.

"How are you?"

He sits down on the bench slowly, leans back to smile, the sun full on his face. "I'm grateful. I'm grateful I survived the night. I'm grateful I'm alive."

"You know what, Gabe? Me too. For both of us."

And he looks at me, and smiles, and I'm grinning. *It's exquisite. Everything. If you think about it Gabe what the fuck are the odds that we'd ever be alive now? And we're only ever going to be alive this once. This once in the history of everything that ever was and will be. And smell that garden and there's this sun full on our faces. And we're here, we're now, and this is. What a fucking thing, Gabe. Look at us.* And I'm laughing and laughing till it hurts and the nurses come out, ask if I'm well. I wave them away, still laughing, grinning over

their shoulders at Gabe, who smiles, and they go back in
to make a note on my chart.

"You shouldn't be talking to Gabe. He's a very sick man."
"So what? He's brilliant, and he's a good guy. He's a great
man."
"You shouldn't encourage him. He's not well."
"Yeah, well never speaking or listening to him isn't
exactly going to get him well, is it? Ignoring him like that,
no wonder he's sad. No fucking wonder he's sick. And
you're supposed to be nurses. You're the mad ones."

She turns away from me before the last sentence is out
my mouth. She murmurs a few words to another nurse,
who writes something down on a chart, and picks up the
phone. I walk as far away as I can. I stand absurdly by the
furthest corner of the fence, get a smoke from someone,
and wait.

✪

There's a tea break before group therapy. I dart in to get a
cup of coffee and Gabe stands by me just long enough to
say in a rushed murmur – "I wanted to say goodbye, and
thank you – for saving my life."

But I'm not sure I heard him right, and I laugh and say, "Shit, Gabe, where're you going? And what do you mean?" But a nurse is nagging at me, "Dear, go to group now. Now. I'll come with you." And Gabe's smiling politely and gone again.

✿

After group, I come back to find Siyanda sitting on the bench. He's a skinny, arrogant little shit, here "for a break, man. What can I say? Overdoing it on the weed yeah but man it's so nice, it's so nice. But my parents, you know how they can be. Eish, so I'm just here to take a break." Every night he asks me the same thing, "Hey, man. There's this philosophical question I'm trying to examine while I'm here, with you guys – you know, I don't know what your sickness is but I'd like to find out while I'm here – Why do some people choose death?" Every night I tell him to fuck off, the little tourist.

He's lounging on the bench, looks up at me, grins, and says, "Hey, Gabe was looking for you."
"Yeah? Where is he?"
"He's gone, man. They transferred him somewhere I think. He said goodbye to me just now. Such a great guy, hey?"

I stand there and stare at him. "He's gone? Where the fuck did he go? Why didn't he tell me?"

"Dude I don't know, man. But he was so nice, said goodbye to me, gave me a hug." He's eyeing me now, waiting for my reaction, "Such a sweet guy, hey? Didn't he say bye to you?"

"Can you shut up for five fucking seconds and tell me where he went? Do you have any idea?"

"Oh, are you upset? Shame, he didn't say bye? He was so, so nice, kept looking for you but he couldn't find you."

I'm standing in front of him with my fist curled and ready before I know what I'm doing. He mock-cowers, glancing at the nurses' station behind me. "Hey! No need to get violent!"

"You pathetic, disgusting little fuck. Get the fuck out of my sight. You disgust me, you spineless fucking kid. Get the fuck out of here."

"You know what'll happen if you actually hurt me."

I can't speak, torn between wanting to vomit and wanting to punch him. I rush to the nurses' station.

"Where's Gabe? Where'd he go?"

"Gabe's been discharged from here, dear. And we told you –"

"Yes I fucking know, but where did he go? Can you give

him a message? I didn't say goodbye to him properly. I needed to tell him stuff."

She pauses a long time, "Look, we told you not to talk to him, he's a very sick man."

"Can you take him a message?"

"Maybe you can give it to the doctor to give to him."

"Alright. I'll do that."

"Wait –"

"What?"

But she thinks better of it, and I go out to sit in the sun by the fence, throw myself into someone else's conversation, sit down by them and smoke my way through a pack.

In about ten minutes, the nurse comes back, stands at my shoulder and holds out a pill. "Dear you're going to take this now. I want you to put this under your tongue."

"Are you serious? Do you really think I'm going to do that? What the fuck for, anyway?"

"You seem very elevated today. Very anxious."

"Of course I'm fucking anxious. One of my friends just left and no-one will tell me anything."

"If you don't put this under your tongue I'm going to have to inject you."

"I'd be really entertained watching you try. Besides, we both know you can't. You're threatening me hoping I'll prefer this to being injected but you can't inject me – not without speaking to the doctor first. And it's a Sunday. Let's see him give enough of a fuck to answer your call."

She walks away. When she isn't back after ten minutes, the pain from my shoulders tensing fades.

⌘

Once on a long trip through the Karoo I watched a crow fly down from a telephone pole and become a man, standing and staring at me as we drove past.

⌘

At dinner there's a different pill in the small cup they give
you with your meal. The nurse doing the meds rounds
stops by me, says, "Take them in front of me please."
"That's not my medication. I take 100mg of Seroquel.
What's that?"
"That's 800mg. Your dose has been raised."
"You can't just do that."
"The doctor wants us to. Take it here please. Take it now."
"You can't be serious."
"Take it or we'll have to put you in High Care."

Aunty Cee looks at me, worried for the first time. She'd
stood shaking and crying when they dragged Zintle to
High Care. I swallow the pills.

Later I pace the fence in the dark, muttering every line of
poetry and humming every song I know, trying to keep
hold of things. I count the bars, the paces. Eventually
I'm leaning on it, staggering, then stumbling. Someone
says "Shame, love, just go to bed. Just let them take you."
And I'm muttering *fuck this fuck it. No.* Until I find myself
on the ground, a rag doll against the fence, neck limp
and eyes still. I'm still there, underneath all of it. I'm
still furious, and screaming there, behind my eyes. But

the line between my mind and body's snapped, and I'm
alone there before I black out, small thing against a fence,
useless and angry, blind and dumb.

⌘

When I was about nine I started seeing a small, pale boy in black who would appear in rooms, always directly in front of me, sometimes blocking me from going through a door, sometimes standing at the foot of my bed. He had his neck thrown back, and his mouth was taut in a scream that didn't make a sound.

✧

When I was around ten or eleven, I started seeing tall shadows around my bed, even when the room was lit. They took the shadows from the corners, from the shapes cast by a coat, or a chair, and made themselves from it. They stood around my bed, breathed slow, watching me, waiting. I started sleeping by my parents, but they followed me. One night my mother stayed up with me, asked are they there? And my breath heaved as I said, yes, *yes yes they're there always.*

✧

Every night for years I would have vivid nightmares that I was being hunted down by a faceless man. I would try to tell my family and friends but they wouldn't believe me, would laugh and say I've always been too riled up. Sometimes they would shake their heads blankly.

Findings

Emma Hauck is thirty years old in February, 1909. She is diagnosed with dementia praecox, now known as schizophrenia, and admitted to the psychiatric hospital of the University of Heidelberg in Germany.

We do not know what her symptoms were. None of the articles and records mention them. We do not know if she heard voices, or saw visions, or believed in things others believed to be nonsensical, which are the most common signs exhibited by those diagnosed with schizophrenia.

She has a husband and two children. Her husband's name is Mark.

The records state that "the outlook improved briefly" resulting in her discharge a month later. Within weeks however, she was readmitted. By August her illness was deemed *unheilbar,* 'terminal, unhealable' and she was transferred to Wiesloch asylum.

She died there eleven years later.

✿

Case study, March 2003, US National Public Radio:

"At the National Institute of Mental Health in Bethesda, MD., one laboratory, run by Dr. Jacqueline Crawley, is home to hundreds of mice that have been genetically altered to mimic the symptoms of people with all kinds of mental problems. Some act anxious – they won't explore exposed areas. Others show a symptom associated with depression – they give up quickly when placed in stressful situations."

The scientists are most excited by the mice they have bred to mimic the symptoms of people with schizophrenia. While it is acknowledged that it is impossible to know what a hallucinating mouse would look like or feel, they have identified a strain of mice whose behaviour, in some ways, approximates a symptom noted in schizophrenic patients – a tendency to startle.

So the scientists at the institute put these mice into a special chamber and play loud tones to see how quickly they flinch. Several of the mice flinch immediately. They are given an antipsychotic medication. It slows the flinching response. The director of the institute is happy. In his interview with NPR he says: "This might mean that the mouse model could be used to test new drugs.

Eventually, it could lead to entirely new ways of treating schizophrenia."

○

Seroquel is an atypical antipsychotic. It is known as SuzieQ on the streets, where it is commonly used as a date rape drug.

○

In the early 1900's, a female psychiatrist, Frieda Fromm-Reichmann, ten years younger than Emma Hauck at the time Frau Hauck is admitted to the Heidelberg asylum, goes on to pioneer the use of psychotherapy as a way of treating "the most serious mental illnesses, like schizophrenia." Though she has trained with Europe's most acclaimed neurologists, Fromm-Reichmann insists that schizophrenia is essentially a condition of abject loneliness, possibly rooted in early experiences of trauma. She asserts that it could, even in its most severe forms, be healed through relationship.

○

The same year Frau Hauck is committed to the asylum in

Heidelberg, doctors at the University of Heidelberg set out to collect what would come to be known as "art brut" – art created by people suffering from some sort of mental illness. The collection includes sculptures, drawings, and poetry, and still does the rounds of museums throughout the world. It came to be known as the Prinzhorn Collection, after Hans Prinzhorn, a student of art history, philosophy, music, and medicine, who first directed the program. During his three-year stay in Heidelberg the collection grew to contain some five thousand items. Roberta Smith, who reviewed an exhibition of the Prinzhorn Collection in New York, April 2000, notes here and there a "beautiful little painting," a "seductive little image". Notes the quaint recurring religious images, the scenes of everyday life, of animals, of work. "Especially impressive is a large drawing by Alfons Frenkl that seems to depict about twenty variations on the iron bit of a bridle."

Smith makes a passing mention of one alcove containing letters. These letters are incoherent in some places, words arranged into columns, repeated over and over till parts of the paper are faded to grey. The letters were written by Emma Hauck. They were never sent. They were found in the archives of the University of Heidelberg and added to the Prinzhorn Collection. They repeat the same phrase,

"Herzenschatzi komm" hundreds of thousands of times. "Sweetheart, come".

The letters are so thickly overlapping as to be illegible in some parts. Some of the hundreds of letters read simply "komm, komm, komm." Come, come, come.

The hospital records show that around the time these letters were written Hauck asked after her family relentlessly. Her husband is noted as "absent".

✿

Almost everyone who comments on the exhibition describes Emma Hauck's letters as "profoundly moving" "heartbreaking," "haunting". Hans Prinzhorn considered the letters an example of "progenital form of drawing" or the "nearest to zero point on the scale of composition".

On the Prinzhorn Collection website, Monica Jagfeld describes the visual composition of the letters as one would a painting. She adds that they are "not really designed for correspondence."

✿

The term "schizophrenia" derives from the Greek roots *skhizein*, 'to split' and *phren*, 'mind'. Medical dictionaries and encyclopedias describe it as being characterized by abnormalities in the perception or expression of reality. It is meant to indicate a fracturing and contradiction of thought and belief, or a lack of appropriate reaction to circumstances. One psychiatrist explained it to me as "Like saying red is a pretty colour when you watch someone bleeding."

In March, 2012, in a psychiatric hospital in Port Elizabeth, South Africa, a fourteen year old girl wanders the corridors of the "Neuro" ward. She asks her fellow patients what language she is speaking. They tell her English. She says she needs another one. She tries again, "What language am I speaking?" The others answer, English. She shakes her head violently and wanders on. She is sent to High Care, where she is strapped to a bed and drugged, after she has set off the fire alarm by following the instructions: "In case of emergency, break glass."

The fence, one night

There's a group of guys on the other side of the fence listening to music on someone's cellphone. I hear Bob Marley's "Redemption Song", and move closer to the fence. Carrie nods her head, "Hmm, now there's some real music, nê?"

A tall coloured guy comes over to the fence with the cellphone playing the song, stands holding it between the bars so we can all listen. We stand there quiet listening to that song, heads bowed. In the dark Carrie mouths the words, a small note making its way out now and then, through the dark.

✣

"I want you to look for the film *Don Juan de Marco*," the doctor said. "Because, my friend, that is the movie of your soul."

"Really? What's it about?"

"About a young man who reminds me so much of you. A romantic. A poet. Passionate. He's just like you really."

I'd been sent home to South Africa from the boarding school in Michigan because of "psychiatric issues". I'd been hallucinating, wandering campus in fevers of alternating mania and terror, living on almost no sleep, writing reams and then nothing at all. Worst was the depression that came with the first November snow, the paralysis of it, the blank fear, the unnamed dread settling over me, pulling me down till I envied the ground the white sleep that had overtaken everything.

They sent me to therapists who posited everything from depression to early onset schizophrenia, though the current favourite was bipolar disorder. I would look at their desks for my cue: a pen with a logo for Lamictal meant bipolar disorder. Wellbutrin for depression. Abilify for psychosis. A simple Astra Zeneca logo meant free-for-all. They loved it. They led me very happily and with great feeling to their pet diagnoses, nodded and taught me vocabularies. Mixed episode, mania, hypomania, depression, rapid cycling, psychosis. So many words, tools. I meant to build a life with them. A story that made sense. For a while I nurtured it, this supposed misfiring of signals in the brain, a tainted mix of chemicals with a pill for every phase of its moods. I was weak and looking for a place to keep me, something to cradle me in. I quoted poetry at them, made them listen to Edith Piaf lose her mind a little at the end of "L'Accordéoniste", watched *Girl, Interrupted*, read Plath, wandered corridors and swallowed the medication and listened to them say, "It's all right, it seems to be the plague of artists. Writers especially." And I thought, let me be maimed like this always, with this writer's plague. Their little wounded sparrow. They will mend me and clip my wings and keep me warm and safe. I will watch the snow from the window.

But little by little the medication took the words, took the gladness of flight from all my thoughts till I could barely string everyday sentences together. It wrapped and wrapped me till I couldn't move. I found that the cage I'd lived in all my life, and only just escaped when I left home to go to art school in Michigan, was only holding another cage, my body, and inside that, another cage, my mind, and what was struggling and fretting, tearing itself to pieces deep down there, was something like my soul, and more than that even – my memory.

I started to rebel, mocking the therapists and fighting the diagnoses, trying to make them understand that madness was preferable to that network of cages, that there was something in it, a summons I was meant to follow. But it was too late. I'd sheltered myself in the system when I thought I was close to killing myself, and now they were determined to keep me. I turned to the poets they'd comforted me with, telling them they could never have written that poetry if they hadn't followed the electric summons of their madness. That there were words, so many words clamoring in every episode, in every misfiring of signals. Something beating under the surface, a hunted animal heart to be freed. They upped the doses. They told me not to fall for the siren song of mania, of absolute freedom. They became more worried about me. They recommended I be sent home for psychiatric assessment.

I was sent to a Dr Meretritz, who let me talk and talk. I was as charming as I could make myself, like a lawyer performing for the judge. I rhapsodized and quoted and tried to make her understand. *Where these words come from, there are more, and more. There are so many things I have to tell. The words I need for it are at the dark heart of the madness, at its electric centre. Let me go there. Let me go.*

When I came out of her office other patients in the waiting rooms stared. My parents asked what on earth I'd said to her – all they'd heard was laughing, sounded like we'd had a grand old time. What had I told her? And I said, "I think she understands. I think she'll understand." She referred us to a colleague of hers, a psychiatrist. It was all going to be fine, I thought, still. Someone understands. I even watched *Don Juan de Marco*.

The psychiatrist, my first, hardly let me get a word in. Shortish, rotund man with a thick Afrikaans accent and no patience for rhapsodizing. We instantly disliked each other, and I shut down, spat out answers designed to annoy him and give him what he wanted by turns. I could see myself losing and became brattish. An obnoxious painting of a cat hung behind his desk. All primary colors and an attempt at abstraction. Every time I tried to explain myself, why I believed the things I did, why I hated the medication, he told me "Ag but that's what all artists say."

Maybe you should start believing them then.

Months later, when I got hold of the letters they'd exchanged, I found he'd provided a provisional diagnosis of a "Mixed Cluster B Type Personality Disorder" as well as "textbook Bipolar II." Dr Meretriz, the one I'd rhapsodized to about truth and beauty and love, who I said had understood, called me a textbook case in her letter – "intelligent and bright, but a textbook case." She was "worried that the medication will stifle her creativity" and referred to my "history of non-compliance." Pat words, laid down like they were all she cared to say about it. I'd flattered and dazzled her, I'd begged prettily. I'd laid out my heart, and she'd smiled, and nodded, and humoured me, then recommended the usual treatment. This one struggles a lot against the medication so make sure you make it stronger. Like I hadn't said anything at all. *Well fuck her*, I thought, *she was just like the rest.* She wished him a merry Christmas. They descended on me like gulls.

⌘

When I was a child, sometimes, as I tried to fall asleep, I'd feel something sweep through me, grand and luminous. I told my mother later it was like God swept me up in an angel's arms. My eyes flew wide open and I felt such piercing joy that I wept.

Such luminous joy came only a few times again as I grew up. Once in front of a concert hall after a friend had played Chopin. The snow was unfurling in the sun. The sunlight shattering a hundred thousand times in your hands, reflecting on the snow till the smallest hidden thing is lit up and luminous, shaken to splendor. That angel brushed past me then. I tried to reach after it but it had gone, and I was left with snow in my hair and a laugh still flying in my throat.

Slowly they left me, those angels. I would see them from a distance, but they didn't come near anymore. I saw them, though, moving through trees or water, watching me from that small distance, looking away, moving on.

Group Therapy

The group session on Friday is on "Rational Thinking." About ten minutes into the session I'm distracted by something in the doorway.

At first there's a shadow, then a blur of red each time I blink. Then the pool of blood spreads. The door is open across from me. The courtyard is just outside that door. In the middle of the spreading blood lies a tawny rabbit with its neck half-bitten through. Its eyes are wide, golden. It twitches and screams. I say *Dear God kill it quick. Please God don't let me make it suffer. Help me kill it quick.* There's blood on my teeth and tongue, the hot reek of blood and that screaming and those eyes. It twitches in the pool of blood and limps towards me. I don't let my eyes leave it for a second.

I rush out the door and hide at the back of the TV lounge, rocking myself calm again, edging away from that maimed thing that won't stop its screaming across the floor, the tiles, the walls, the glass.

A nurse comes out and asks, "Are you all right sweetheart?"

And I am held to her, and she talks to me like I'm her

own child. Like a child I press myself against her and cry, contained. Thinking *No, no why, don't you dare be kind when you are what you are.* Mute with sobs. Futile and small, raging with my small fists.

Three days later she tells the head counsellor, who changes me to another group and ups my medication. I stand straight as I can, and solemn as a wronged child I tell her to go to hell, *I knew no-one could be trusted here.*

The girl with the long straight hair and a collection of sparkly barrettes stands by her window for two hours, because her boyfriend's coming to visit today. Carrie and I wait with her, watch every car for a dark blue Honda saying he'll be next, he'll be next. When his car pulls into the parking lot she breathes, "That's him, that's my boytjie. Ag, isn't he handsome?" And Carrie and I smile for her, say yes he is, lucky girl. She rushes to the door of the ward, she's not allowed any further, and hides behind one of the doors so she can jump him when he walks in. He walks in carrying cheap daisies and the whole fucking world on his shoulders. She grins like a child and jumps at him, wraps her arms around him. He jumps and looks sheepish, mutters something to greet her. She holds onto his arm, beaming as they walk the long corridor to the nurse's station to sign the visitors' register.

Carrie and I duck back into the room, shy suddenly. I'm ashamed of how we're shy, how we stand straighter, straighten our clothes, wipe our eyes to look more awake, shake his hand with grips like a vice. He doesn't meet our eyes, but smiles. It's pained but it's good enough for her, and all afternoon I watch them from behind the fence, in the shadow of the smokers' corner, making my way through a pack as they walk round the garden again, and again. She smiling like a child, her head on his shaking shoulder, as if with every turn she's forgetting, sleeping sound.

Sweetheart, come

I am told that the Greek term *phren,* besides meaning 'mind,' means 'heart.' *Schizein* – 'broken.' *Phren* – 'heart.' Schizophrenia therefore comes to mean, 'broken-hearted.'

When I went mad at 17 I was in the rarefied air of Michigan's north woods, in a school like Neverland. We'd been brought there and paid for, making art day in and out, dancers and sculptors and violinists and writers. Wunderkinder wondrous and sad as thoroughbred horses run till the constant flight, the pistol shot saying *Now, now this second!* wore us to sinew. I fell in love there with so many people, though we were all children. They came a little way into the madness with me, but never completely, for which I am still thankful.

✿

There was magic in it, they said. Something moving quicker, truer in the skin and the blood. We called it madness but what it was, was love.

✿

One night Theo said, "I wish I could take some of it into me, to take it away from you."

I said, "No, don't you dare, I'd never wish this on anyone. Beloved, don't you dare."

"But maybe then I could come with you," she said.

All that night and for many afterwards I sat up beside her bed, muttered feverish into the dark at the voices, *You touch her and I will tear you apart. Don't you ever dare touch her. I will tear you vein from vein.*

But they were not the ones with veins, I was. They lived in my veins. They were air again as soon as you tried to touch them.

✿

For most of fall and winter we wrote reams, fueled by our fervor and long nights shaking with music in the overheated dusky rooms. Sometimes we just clutched each other, naked as if in search of something defined, sure and earthbound, chaste as animals are chaste, moved by blood-currents.

✿

She said with her sharp teeth at my throat that sometimes, when it happens, God help her, I am beautiful to her. "God help you," I said. "God help me."

✪

I have to believe that it was beautiful. Everything alive at once in the blood, nothing ignored, nothing meaningless.

Everything mattered, everything was grand and sweeping. For the first time in my life I could believe that the death of a sparrow could be mourned by the entire world. It all became dear to me in a moment. Everything proved to be made with perfect symmetry, such form and grace and loveliness in how it moved, how everything moved and was alive and part of the same grand flow of everything. The divine lit up in my lungs. Every day painted electric with prophecy. The stars shattered and moving. Every vein a river. All the angels of God fiery in the blood. Nothing ignored, nothing to be outdone.

I walked the night streets talking faster than anyone could follow, threw money into the air and bought my friends everything they wanted and what they didn't want and what none of us could afford. I thought I could buy up the world. And we were going to start a revolution to crusade for the rights of everyone who ever experienced pain and we had unravelled a philosophical theory that could explain the world, had mapped it on five A3 sheets of paper one afternoon in an empty classroom, when the dappled leaves moving on the windows said, *Yes, yes, you. You know it now*. It all moved and fitted into each other perfectly, whole, entire, everything whole. That was the grand and vital difference that flew in the face of everything every day, the cruelty and the war and the suffering. Here was everything swept up at once, and nothing, not a mote of dust, not a glance or a second without meaning.

☼

"Of course you're needlessly dramatic. Living life like it's a book."
Books are life, just more articulate, I tell them. What else do you do with this life that is so vastly unprecedented.

Another says to me "I don't see any greatness there, only you very, very sad."
I hate that word. It droops. I hate it because it pats down and dry the splendour. Better the words that indicate a wound sustained.
Pain. Agony. Hurt. Even the child's lisped and lonesome

sore. A wound. I used to cut myself so that the word I used could match their understanding of it.

✧

In those times I'd thought I could captivate them, take them with me to make them see the splendour of what I was always reaching for, the brilliant transcendent thing that roared out of every atom of the world. I thought they were with me in the enchantment. They held me, stroked my hair, called me their silly love, their darling mad one, *shot of whiskey, cigarette stolen and smoked in the sun behind the birch trees. Fox with its tail in the mud. On the run. Poor lover.*

A love of mine, Sonya, wrote about me running from a thousand debts, small demons and worries bright and apparent on my shoulders. She wrote about the night I took them all to a café, told them to buy everything, anything. They were too modest, pressed me to save the money – it was all I had for two months. One hundred dollars. No one would take it from me, standing there in the lamplight, pressing it into their hands, talking at a gallop about the grand accessibility of things, and so I threw it into the air. We could buy up the world, right now, why wait, why save, why be careful of or for anything? Everything was ours. Everything was brilliant.

Choose whatever you want my loves, take it. Take what you want. It's yours before you even ask.

When she wrote about that night, she said she
"would not touch
what Darling held like fire."

It was a beautiful poem that made a lot of people angry; they claimed it wasn't her story to tell, that she was romanticizing things. I read it years after the fact, on the other side of the world. I wonder at how she saw that blood-debt that hung on me like a red coat. I saw every night painted electric with prophecy, and she saw me standing worn out in the rain, the words spent, whatever wealth I had scattered in the dirt. My hands empty.

✿

Sometimes in the worst of it I remembered the first girl I loved, Theo, who breathed the blue smoke into me. She called me beautiful, once. A beautiful woman called me beautiful. Such things do happen. They were going to tie me to the hospital bed and inject me. My face was scratched and my snot was running all over the place and I was crying in the bathroom because I couldn't walk properly and I was just so fucking tired of it. Sound curling in my throat, hurt dog. But she held me to lie down gentle in her lap far away, and gave me water, and turned the lights down, and we lay there together, and she called me beautiful in her arms. It happens sometimes. The miracle rises mad in your lungs. She pulled my hands from my face and stroked where I'd clawed at myself.

She said, *shh, shh. My beautiful love.* Those are words she said. She said, "Remember the bluejay." *That February day holding everything still and on the shore a bluejay flew up in impossible blue from the trees.*
"Yes, always remember that."

That November I had tried to read the writing the branches made across the sky. I thought if I could decipher them I'd understand the lost key to everything. The explanation and redemption of the whole world. I told her so but the words stumbled, broke into sounds that would not arrange themselves, and the whispering from the air and the writing I could not read drowned me out.

That one day she brought back to me, lying in her arms, the branches were quiet against the sky, and I was beautiful, too. My love followed me into the night and I held her in the frosted air. I leaned close and pointed, said

There are angels there, unfurling in the streetlamp light. There in the snow is where they are. They beat their wings along the roads.

She let me talk. She stood with me. I watched them such a long time. Everyone calls you in eventually, and my legs give in. But I have been held by hands I am too weak to praise enough.

This was my only dignity, that even my mind was once a lovely thing. On those blank days locked in white rooms I would lie on the bed, my mind trembling through my body, bleeding from a hundred invisible cuts. I once heard about a boy who ran through a glass door, and died on the ground outside, bleeding and laughing a little, at the impossibility of it. My mind felt rarified, made of glass, but once it was loved. The fractured windowpane, the kaleidoscope broken, blood-debt to the old rituals, synapses fraught and filled with wings and breath as the window is, from which a woman jumps to her death, again and again. Someone saying, *She became a bird.*

☼

Of all of them one was the dearest. I woke up one morning to find their names lit in my lungs, and the words *Thank you God, for making them. Thank you for them in this world* on my mouth.

We would go out to the woods in the snow to fight. We fought earnest as children, a deadly edge to every blow, twisting at and with each other, a fine red thread between us like a prelude to dancing or love.

Some crazy thing was beating its way through my lungs wanting that taste of blood on my tongue to have a reason.

Once we left a deep cut on the exact same spots on each other. When the mark she left healed, months later, I sobbed till my throat was raw.

✿

At the age of fourteen Emily Bronte was bitten by a mad dog in the village. Without a word she strode home and into the kitchen. Taking up one of the Italian irons from the fire, she applied it directly to sear the bitten place, without a word or sound, so as not to frighten anyone.

We found words for this in the Bronte sisters, with their little raw soul amongst them.

✿

Lovers search for signs. Every day is lit up with the prophecy of small things. Anything will do. One afternoon I watched her map out the northern constellations with spilled salt on a dining table.

✷

We were drawn too close to the Brontes. Something about the bleakness, the wind, the world like knives cutting through us, always too keen. Every touch as pain.

Of Branwell, the near-forgotten brother so far fallen in the world, James Parton wrote in 1886: "He returned to his home a desperate man. His dissipation, formerly secret, now became open and reckless; he drank and took opium; he was violent and childish by turns, raving of his lost mistress one moment and threatening suicide the next.

The stronger Emily pitied him, and did not shrink from giving him her assistance and companionship even in his worst moments, when he was scarcely less than a madman."

✷

We were both children. We would climb trees, fight in the snow, play loup-garou in the lamplit winter nights.

Every lover I've had has ruffled my hair and called me their loup-garou, when I am weak from what happens. Each one of them had a language we tried to reach each other in.

✧

In the language of the Hmong, the term for epilepsy translates to: "the spirit catches you and you fall down."

A German woman told me she loved English for the term 'to fall in love'. "As if that is it, it is done. I am fallen and nothing to be done. I am fallen and love catches me." She blushed as she said it.

My love and I took our shape shifting from Greek.

When I told her I loved her, I was drunk with it, murmured to her in a dark cupboard where we'd holed up with six other people one April night to tell stories. I told her in every language I knew. The words were drunk in the dark, and I thought *Now be the gentlest you ever were with this the dearest thing you've found.* And I kissed her in the corner of her mouth, gentle for the first and the last time. Her breath drew in quick and sharp in the dark.

From then on it was French and German, Arabic and Russian. When we were on either side of the Atlantic, so much still unsaid, (I am told there is some delicate metaphor in Greek that mentions the last dregs in the wineskin). I looked for her in Greek. Our definitions met and came alive in it.

Androgyne.

Kairos.

Amymon – a Homeric epithet meaning beautiful
in the way a warrior ready to fight is beautiful.
When I was crippled with losing her I still flourished
in Ancient Greek. I fell asleep surrounded by cards of declensions and words I wanted to send her one by one, saying
here you are, here, and here. I am learning.

✿

She was obsessed with monsters. Medusa the Gorgon was the one she loved most. I used to resent that at times, thinking *what could you ever understand about ugliness?*

She had stern seawater eyes when she stared things down.

She had a way of doing that – when I told her sometimes about things – of staring down the dark thing that rose up. I have never seen or been seen like that again.

When I stumbled through those first passages in Greek I wrote one out on a slip of paper. I held it till it became illegible: *I came back from that country and said that I had seen the Gorgon, but it did not make me a stone.*

✿

I took her aside and asked her *Are you sure*. I showed her the scars. I told her to think long and hard. She was solemn and upright, she turned from me and I waited.

I do not remember a moment of that day that was not spent in prayer.

In the afternoon I went to sit with friends at lunch. I ate nothing, only searched every face and grinned each time I jumped at a sudden noise. All the languages undone around me. There were huge windows and the sun dazzled me. No one knew.

Out of nowhere, out of the dazzle of sun, as if out of the sunsplit windows she ran up to me, she flew at me, all legs, arms, savage chest, holding me, a flurry of words in French and German saying *Yes. She's thought she's tried so hard to say no but she's sure she's sure she loves me. She has to go now her mother is expecting her but Yes. Yes.*

And she ran off, and I sat there and grinned and grinned like a fool, and the sun beat through the windows over the lake, and reflected on everything, dazzled off the chairs and the cutlery and the faces of all the incredulous friends who hadn't understood a word, only seen her rush at me, hold me, kiss me once for a second only half-brushing my lips, and they looked at me, looked at me grinning there, king of the earth that spring, and never again.

✿

Kissing in the Chapel Garden. In the stairwells. In closets. By the lake.

All our sweet sunlit rooms open to the wind. It tangles the curtains. It topples the things of glass and porcelain. It moves the sheets.

Love, love, no one on earth can dare say they are happier than I am now.

You are the first rest of my life. You are what I delight in.

We lay in bed and I told her, "Really, what better form of worship is there for the one who made us, than loving, loving you as much as I do?"

She smiled and looked up through the windows at the leaves. The shadows moved over her.

We listened to Marlene Dietrich sing *Ich bin von Kopf bis Fuß auf Liebe eingestellt,* and I looked at her and said, "What are you thinking?" She stretched like a cat and said, "I feel like a painting." I told her, *You are. You are.*

✧

She is not there. Somewhere the little raw soul slipped out in the early morning, tangle-haired, poetry still taut in her throat, wary. Me on the other side of the door, saying *love, love.* Till my throat is raw with it.

✧

"Most of the time I am just afraid for you, love."
"Don't be."
"You know it's no good saying that. I just worry about

you all the time. I can't do this anymore."

I begged hard. "Love, we'll steal time."

"What a lovely idea – to steal time. But what happens between now and then?"

We hold fast.

"I'm sorry, Liebe, it's just the in between that kills me."

☼

Emily Bronte at fourteen striding straight-backed into the kitchen, to sear the place where the mad dog bit her, without a word.

☼

"Branwell grew worse and worse, his sufferings and paroxysms more and more terrible, until, in 1848, the end came. By a last strange exercise of will he insisted upon meeting his death standing. He died erect upon his feet, after a struggle of twenty minutes."

☼

Something came in with me then, a dog at my feet. On the long nights we sit beside each other. This dog and I. Somewhere where the wound was made she must have slipped out, a shadow, and now follows at my heels, waiting to live in my marrow again.

○

I have been told I am loved for how like a dog I am.

"The thing about dogs is they always have this terrible sadness deep in their eyes." – This from another love, Satine, who left me, specifying the dog I am as feral.

I told her, "It's because dogs know, deep down, that they will always love you."

○

A year later, when I tell her how I fell from a horse at a gallop, how I laughed and laughed, lying in the mud and shit, on the other side of a fence.
I don't remember crashing through, how I couldn't walk for two days (I meant it to be a funny anecdote for her to laugh at.)
She says horrified, "You idiot, you stupid bastard," and I laugh like I did at the horse, say *Don't worry about me, I can't die yet. Not yet.*

"Yes I'm sure you'll go down in a blaze of glory when you do. Till then, you need a nurse."

"I don't want a bloody nurse. You know that."

She laughed at me,

"You're an idiot. A delightful idiot."

And you're mine, she completed it, on a June day, years ago now, *all mine.*

✿

One day, years after, lying in someone else's arms

I said to her

Love I want you to remember me

as I was when I was

luminous. Alright?

She kisses my hair, says nothing. Satine,

the one who stayed the longest,

who had come too late.

Remember the time I grabbed you by the waist

and kissed you in the street, and that van full of policemen

applauded. Remember me climbing

over the balcony naked to fetch the laundry

off the line. Remember me shouting

ridiculous things in the rain. Remember me young

and stupid. I have such love in me. Remember that.

The one who stood rarefied with it,

in Cape Town, Paris, the Storms River Mouth, the shore

of Wahbekaness, Puget Sound. Who claimed
everywhere as ours.

Suddenly I was speaking,
delirious, to every love of mine: Remember the one
who gave you her jacket
in December, said my blood was hot enough,
that I was mad with you, that I rose in my love
electric. The idiot who kissed you
always too hard. Crowed
with the triumph of you.

Remember me staying up night after night
by your bed, the dog who followed you, slept
on the floor at your side.
Promised you the Nile, and Siberia. Remember
the Betsy Bay Inn, you running through the sunlit rooms,
the white curtains, saying look at this one, look!
And me saying *Pick one, pick one. We'll live here forever.*
The spring wind off Lake Michigan setting your hair
tangled against the dunes and the sky and the water. Me
undressing and diving into the snowmelt, thinking of
you, always you the shadow dancing on my open arms.
Remember how I swore I'd come back,
in time for another spring.

I'm grown up, love – I cry, a small thing, worn out,
I'm used up and weighed up
and wanting – I am digging my nails into
whatever will keep me. Remember me how I was
when I was arrogant
with the stain of you on my mouth. Remember
the frosted grass
and you barefoot, running beside the bus
when they sent me away. Oh love. I'm lonely here
on the far side of everything. I was only young that once.

Satine stroked my hair, lovely neglected one,
who found me already haunted,
and shuddered when I called out to
all the other loves I've had, and she was patient.
I shuddered and seized as it came again
and again, the grip on my throat
and ribs, the hundreds of dark birds
in the corner of the room, and my brother
standing there. I shouted at him, I grinned,
taste of blood staining my teeth,
lips in shreds, and my laugh s
hook loose from me
like rust. You bastard. Wait for me, you bastard.
Can't you see I'm busy?

"Who are you talking to, love?"

My brother, my poor brother. That bastard, my poor brother, my son, love –

And there's no end to it now. I crumple against her, shake like a child. *My poor brothers and my loves, all of them caught and pinned and hurt and why love I keep saying don't you hurt him don't hurt any of us love why where did we come from and where did it come into us and why. They hurt you and tear you out and why love tell me they hurt us they hurt us I still wake up some nights –*

"I know, love. You're safe, you're safe."

I wake up some nights saying *be kind. Please be kind to me* – those words shook out of me.

And my brother stood there, and said nothing. And he has no name. We have the same breath and blood.

She saw none of it. She held me down through the seizing and wiped the sweat from my forehead,

brought me water, wiped away the shameful things –

the snot and the tears,

took the knife from the bedside,

and hid it so well I still haven't found it.

She said, "I have years in me yet."

Three days later she left in the late afternoon, me staggering through the door, too worn out to stop her, or lie. When we slept together again, months later, I was racked by something shrieking in my lungs, a gale driving itself down my throat, setting my hands shaking round the knife, and when I held it above her, she looked up at me and said, come back to me now. Come back to the world. The knife fell and I lay with her for so many evenings, and she stroked my hair, hands small and gracious in the dark. She stayed a long time and was the most betrayed of all of them. My words never saved a thing.

☼

I've survived it. I still walk.
There was salt at the door and sage burning in the small hours.
I stood there electric
while it happened. Sometimes they stand with me.
Their names are a fixation in my blood.

☼

Branwell, the lover and madman, stood up to die.

And when I was very little I sat transfixed in front of a picture of a surgical incision under a scan – the blue parted by the scalpel to give way to fire beneath the skin.

The wound shining. I walked around certain we were all reining in fire under our skins.

These are the stories that make us. I walked with a love along a road in autumn fiery with bougainvillea. I told her Joseph Banks, the 25-year-old botanist on the *Endeavor*, paced the deck when they could not disembark onto the shores of South America, a continent they'd never charted, spread for them, unnamed. Imagine that, I said, to step onto land new to you and name it. He would escape every night, swim to the shores of Rio de Janeiro, to steal the bougainvillea that now lit up the road, midges like embers flying from them. She asked me, "How do you remember all this?"

I said to her, "I remember everything I've ever loved."

She knew all the Northern Stars and mapped them in salt on a table. *If you love something, learn it by heart.*

When Van Gogh was kept in the asylum at St Remy, he painted the stars from memory.

In 15th century Japan, the shogun Ashikaga Yoshimasa sent a broken tea bowl away to China to be repaired. It was returned to him held together with metal staples, and, disgusted by the ugliness of the mending, he sought to find a way to repair broken pottery that would still be pleasing to the eye. He added gold dust to the adhesive resin. The cracks were lined in gold, and the broken pottery was made more beautiful by emphasizing the break. The art is known as kintsugi.

☼

"I hear Japanese warriors would test the blade of their sword by letting a silk veil fall across it. If the silk is split, the blade is ready."

My friend smiles. She and I are talking about love in a bar in Cape Town, years later, neither of us whole, every old story told between us, just this once. She's escorting me to a conference, reporting my health to our friends back in Grahamstown, *Meds taken, coordination still bad. Speech ok. Memory ok.*

"It's probably bullshit, but what an idea. Something exquisite coming out of fire, put in and brought back from fire, again and again. And at the end, love, at the end – the test is gentle. It's silk falling. It's letting silk fall."

She sighs heavily, looks away. "Ja, such are God's ways."

I grab her hand. She blinks, mouth pulling quiet. I have never wanted to be believed so much when I say this, "You are going to split the silk clean in two."

☼

I have lined the break with gold. If you find yourself in a far place, and poor, take me with you. There is enough gold in me to buy you an empire. Buy it. Buy up the world, my love. It is yours before you ask.

"It's exactly the same as last time, isn't it? Hey ma? It's only six years ago."

They rush into the ward, flanked by two nurses. A smallish woman, pale and bewildered, accompanying her son, a tall man in his late twenties with a shock of washed out blond hair. His mother's eyes are such a pale shade of blue they are almost silver. He has her eyes. They sit him down, his mother pulled aside to fill out a form. Another woman, with the same build as the mother but with dyed dark hair, sits near them, covering her mouth and murmuring something now and then, presumably to comfort. I sink further into the corner of the dining room, where I can watch all this. We hear a child's scream from the end of the corridor. Carnia. A nurse comes back, "Sorry, sir. We were just dealing with an aggressive patient."

"An aggressive patient?"

Nurse nods, and his mother stares ahead, away from both her son and the room at the end of the corridor. The dark-haired woman murmurs "aggressive patient" absently and turns to look round. When she sees me she starts, and looks away. As they take her son's blood pressure she stares at one of the paintings.

His eyes are half-closed. Pale, drugged. Pupils pinpricks. He murmurs softly to the nurse in broken isiXhosa. He keeps asking for reassurance whenever she checks something. "That's good, eh? Isn't it?"

He keeps turning to his mother, "This is just the same as last time, ma. Eh?"

His eyes are vacant. He's gone.

His aunt's name is Debbie. Yellow shirt, denim jacket. Permed dark hair. She seems to do all the talking. When the others go to an examining room she turns to me, slowly. Looks me up and down, then launches into everything, tells me how difficult things have been. The violence ("not like him, you know. Jon's such a sweet boy when he wants to be") the drugs ("Cocaine, you know. Tik. Dagga obviously. I don't know what else"). Tears up.

"Are you a patient?"
"Yeah… Yeah."
"Ag shame man."
She looks me up and down.

"Ag, it's ok. C'est la vie, you know."

"Mhmm. How long you been here?"

"A week."

"Ag."

"Yeah."

✿

When he's drugged enough they let him walk the ward. He stumbles to the TV room where we all try to pay attention to the TV, or each other, if only to block out the nurses. When he talks he talks about the stars, his dog. The drugs and the crime and how fucking long he spent in prison too, but mainly the stars and his dog and his girlfriend. He knows so many constellations, and he talks about sleeping in the back of a bakkie with her under the stars near Durban, with the waves crashing. "I need my girl. She says 'Love you lots'. She sends me an sms saying 'love you lots'. How'm I supposed to feel, man? Ek's seer, man. I'm sore."

He and Joseph swap prison stories for a while, but he stops, looks away for a while, blinking. "I've seen a lot, man. There's so much shit to see."

Joseph tells us about the time he saw a puppy dragged

along on a chain. Jon looks close to tears. It seems almost ridiculous, this tough man so deeply wounded. "Ag no, no." He wails like a child. "Don't tell me these things. You don't know. I've got a soft heart, man. I've got a soft heart."

Our side is known as "Neuro" to the nurses, "Lost City" to the patients. Just as "Clinical," the ward for "the hopeful cases" is called "Sun City" by the patients. During visiting hours everyone in Lost City slinks off to corners, the ones with visitors all going to the TV room, speaking in whispers like *They* can hear. I sit behind the pillar by the smokers' corner, trying to stay out of sight because some of the visitors get creeped out by me, the tangled-haired girl with the three broken earrings and three talismans round her neck. I do try to smile but no-one meets my eye, so I try not to fuck up their visit and sit in my corner, listening to Bob Dylan or Beethoven and trying a new brand of cigarette every day. Menthol days are the worst.

One day this little girl, a toddler still, swaying away from her mother's hand, trying to strike out on her own comes to the fence where I'm sitting and laughs. Four milk teeth, dark eyes and hand reaching through the fence. I don't know what to do with my face, thinking God, God. She doesn't care at all, is so completely unaware of the way things are here. I crouch by the fence, hold out my hand and she grabs it. She grabs my hand through that fence beaming at me. I glance at her mother, standing

there tight lipped with a grip on the child's other hand.
What's her name, ma'am?
"Gabriella." The mother's hand twitches in her child's.

Still that small insistent hand reaching through the fence
toward me, and those bright eyes and that grin. I shake
her hand with a solemn nice to meet you. "Gabriella, hey
love, hey, Gabriella baby. What a lovely name. Do you
know you have the name of an angel?"

She reaches her hand to me again, and with such a
desperate, bounding joy in me I have the nerve to kiss it
gently. She lets out one ringing "Hah!" And her mother
is politely pulling her back towards the visitors' tables.
Gabriella's hand doesn't make it through the fence, and
I step back, torn between my pride, my politeness, and
wonder at this small thing reaching to me here. But I step
back. *If I show anything more of that joy in my throat, if I hold
onto her hand and laugh and smile and coo at her, desperately, as
I want to, I'd be proving them right. That I'm mad and starved
from loneliness.* So I leave her hand reaching back for me,
and stand watching her go.

I walk inside, stop by the nurse's station. Ask when's the
soonest I can see the doctor, as something works itself to
a frenzy in my ribs.

Swallow

A missed dinner date with some girl with her cheap cigarettes and her Regency erotica, staring at your tragic hands trembling on the buttons of your black coat so apt for tragedy and *Didn't you spend time in an asylum,* she asks, *what for?*

People like to tousle your hair, pet you. They compare you to a tame fox. That's all well and good till you piss on their rugs and chew up their furniture and bite them on the neck when you make out. *Then you'll throw me out, won't you love? Or take me to a shelter and hope for the best, right, love? Right, darling?* They laugh.

You feel like a cliché. You run because you've got a lunch date with a woman who dresses like a Victorian and makes you laugh in that way that dredges up the old guilt. You run and on the way jack some old lady's pink roses so you don't show up empty-handed.

She stands in a group of people, laughing and talking, lipstick smile and red ribbon round her throat. She has kohl lining her eyes and thanks you in French for the roses. Her friends smile and wave and go, and you're sitting with her at the window with tea and some chocolate thing that makes her groan. She makes you think of Helena Bonham Carter. You tell her, and she thanks you. She talks and makes you laugh so much you feel guilty, almost feel the hand on your shoulder and the Ativan under your tongue and the last ragged dash before the defeat. Now and then she's quiet because she thinks you want to say something and you do, you do. But now you think of it *is she really there* and *isn't this cafe so many panes of coloured glass turning on itself like clockwork* and she's smiling at you with those eyes and that sweet tongue gone still for your sake. And the waitress is staring and your napkin is in shreds and you can't fill that silence so she goes on talking because she's kind. She's one of those kind ones.

You know your mouth's pulled down and taut on your left side, you know it makes you talk funny, makes your smile a crooked gash across your face, carnivalesque. But she loves the carnival, she says. And now you think you love her. She takes you to the children's graveyard up the hill by the Botanical Gardens where you crouch by the grave of a three year old named William, where she darts among the graves in a red coat. You crouch down and touch the stone wind-worn and bereft. She says its wuthering up here, and it is, grey sky and the trees standing ragged in the wind, leaves falling. You think to yourself there is a child's body under my hand, deep down. And if there's one thing in all your strange life you have never doubted the sanctity of, it's children. You tell her so without stuttering. She will look at you with kind eyes. You will walk down again to the town, walk the windblown streets to your house alone. You will lie in your garden till night falls watching leaves fall and thinking about Alice Liddell and the girl who had her eyes.

That's when you know you're going crazy, so you go back inside and pick up the whining cat belonging to the neighbours, named Rasputin because the fucker keeps coming back and pissing on your vegetable patch. You silence his protests with a *nyet* and *da svidanya,* watch him slink off through the gate, his ice-blue eyes resentful and inarticulate.

The guy with the ice-blue eyes dead and gone had threatened to kill anyone who – and here he was restrained and medicated so you're not sure what you're not supposed to do if you want to live. You feel kind of bad for him because he gets teary when his girlfriend sends him texts saying luv u lots and when your new friend Joseph talks about how he once saw a puppy dragged along on a chain. You tell no one that feeling kind of bad is tearing your heart out with crying for him and every other fuckup at the second before the meds hit and they're ghosts again, comrades who died long ago.

Joseph the ex-everything addict is tall and shares his Camels with you and laughs at all the right people. He gives you recommendations on tattoo artists in Grahamstown and promises to bring you a box of fly fishing equipment he found at a dump. His hands and mouth are serious as he talks about fishing, names all the best spots in the Eastern Cape. You never see him again because no one calls each other after that place. But you do walk up the cul-de-sac past the old people with their sad Maltese yapping on their porch, to the studio in the backquarters of someone's house. The artist you get is jumpy and speaks in funny voices because he fucking can and it's fucking funny, right? He thinks you're cool because he overhears you telling your housemate that we need to return *Fantastic Mr Fox* to the rental place. You like him. He tattoos a fox on your breast and a swallow on your wrist while Flogging Molly plays in the background. Says how fucked up his back is and fuck what'll be so good right now is some rum. He asks what the fox means, but not the swallow. There's no need to ask, between the two of you. Swallows were for sailors who had sailed five thousand nautical miles. That's a fucking long way. The ocean is one huge trembling, one huge breathlessness. The collection of everything that kills, everything already in you, water and salt and an aching for air. Swallows are for ex-prisoners who get them after release.

Sometimes more than one is needed. In the shower you look at it and remember. Someone drops something in the kitchen and you jump, shoulders taut and shivering as bird wings in that way that drives your violin teacher crazy. You've taken up the violin, thinking *maybe this, maybe if I lean into this hard enough they'll hear me, they'll know*. You look at the ink swallow and almost ask aloud when it's going to be true. You almost ask that swallow flying up your veins when it's going to mean something aloud. But you don't. They might hear.

On the day my friends have promised to visit me I get up two hours early, spend an hour agonizing over what to wear, how to act, training myself to stand straighter, not look at the ground so much, seem more awake, even laugh. At last I go to sit up straight-backed on the bench in the garden, counting prayer beads, ready. I wait for three hours.

They come in all smiles, asking after me at the nurses' station. I try to walk out to greet them before being fetched. I grin and mutter hello's through my teeth saying, "Let's get the fuck out of this place they're all fucking crazy." And they laugh and hurry me out the door. On our way out Jon stops us and asks if we can get him a pack of Princetons. We shout sure and we're in the car and out of that place. We only have a few hours.

The sheer strangeness of being outside, away, makes me skittish as a frightened hare. Everything is heightened, everything seems to come at me from every angle. When my father drove me here, we stopped at the beach before I had to be admitted. He asked if I wanted to get out and walk around a bit, and I said no. Instead I sat in the passenger seat, staring at the sea, and hating every second of it. I'm not sure why. I've always had the worst pride. Even when I was little I hated to be told what to do, I hated to know that a locked door wasn't mine to open, that I could be kept anywhere against my will. The worst was always the indulgence of whoever kept me -- I'd spit in their face before accepting their charity. They never mention how humiliating it is, being mad.

My hands shake more than usual. I stutter. I lose track. Before I understand what's happening we're at a table. The menu at the restaurant confuses me. Lyra asks if I need help and I mutter no, it's alright. I know too keenly how I'm failing, how reading a menu is enough to send my head spinning. Shame has that grip at my throat and I get up, excuse myself, the words rough on my tongue, rattling clumsily like dice. "Shall I go with you?"

"No. No, love, it's alright."
I wander around, completely bewildered at all this. A shopping mall. All I want is the fucking bathroom but it takes walking in circles, going down an escalator, getting lost there, going up again, asking a sales assistant, going down the escalator again, and finding the woman's bathroom at the end of a corridor with too many turns, where some men are doing maintenance work. They stop their painting to stare at me, but I can't stop my

hands shaking or my head and face twitching. One of them whispers to another. I'm muttering, *Idiot. Fucking idiot. It's a fucking mall. Christ can you not even find the bloody bathroom? God. God. God.*

I feel like I've worn His name out for myself in these past few years.

I reach the bathroom. I don't know what to do with myself, really. I have a vague idea that I came here to cry, or collect myself. I can't cry, though. I try. I grasp the basin, dig my nails into my palm, close my eyes and remember, remember everything, think of everything. But I can't. Still, even my reflection sets my heart pounding. The mirrors, with lights above and below, the gleaming metal, the porcelain.

An old woman, prim and neat in pearls and floral blouse, comes in and shoots me a worried look. I dodge out the door before it swings shut.

As I navigate my way back to the restaurant, I map out the lines of logic I need to get through the next couple of hours, holding conversation with my friends, making sure their visit isn't wasted. I want to cry when I look at them, having driven all that way for me, just to see me. I feel all the debts of my life settle at my shoulders.

I hold it together enough to talk at the table. I sense the slight pause they give me, the constant benefit of the doubt as my words come out garbled, sometimes. As I stare now and then, lost. When the bill comes I insist I'll pay for everyone. They're all horrified, adamant that I shouldn't, they're here to take me out. "You did, though. You have. You came all this way. You came all this way and you didn't even have to. Let me do one thing for you at least. What the fuck am I going to buy in a psych ward? What the fuck else will I spend this month's money on?"

The argument goes on just a little too long, crossing over into being uncomfortable. I take out my bank card and grip the bill. They stare at me and one says "Honey, don't. Stop that right now. We're here to take you out. Don't be like this."

I'm ready to scream. *You didn't have to come here and look at me I'm disgusting I'm ugly and stupid and they've fucked me up you guys I can't tell you how but I'm this small ugly thing and I can't even read the stupid fucking menu why do you have to help me all the time can't you just let me pay for your fucking meal at least. Give me this one dignity. I love you and you came all this way and look at how little I am and how little I have to thank you with. Give me this one small dignity.* But the words get lost on my tongue somewhere, roll uselessly in my mouth as I hand over the bill.

They never talk about these things when they talk about going mad.

☼

When we got back to the car I told them about the screams you hear there. I don't know what I said exactly, only that I kept thinking *That sound, that sound no one understands what you see there, what it is.* I don't even know I'm saying it all out loud till I feel hands on mine, Liz holding my hand, and Lyra with her arm round me, and them sitting there, quiet, listening. Knowing now.

When we get back to the hospital I blurt out, "Fuck I don't want to go back" before I realize how ungrateful that must sound. We stop for a second in the parking lot. There's a sweep of grass by it, a grassy slope ending in a fence thickly overgrown with morning glories. Purple and white. Liz looks at me, looks at the grass, and says right, we're going to run.

"What? No we're not." For a second something leaps up

and says *Holy shit we're finally going to make a run for it.* But I realize she means just down the slope, into the grass, and I'm sullen, resigned. I've become my own jailer. But then she's got her hands on her hips and a schoolgirl grin and the grass is bright in the afternoon and I am *not inside.* And that's what everything becomes, the simple fact of *not being inside.*

And she says, "Yes we are. Come on."
We hurl ourselves down the slope, roll down it, lie in the grass. We pick morning glories and put them in each other's hair. I try to make Lyra a crown of them, gather the loveliest ones I can find to twine in her blonde hair. All around us in this impossible corner where everything's overgrown, there is purple and white nodding where the light is green. All the while Lyra takes pictures. When I lie down in the grass I close my eyes, and they're sitting and standing around me, my loves, and I think let me stay here, let me lie down easy here. A year later Lyra will give me a drawing of me lying in the grass there, just as she photographed it, with the words "Only love" above it.

Someone settles down into the grass beside me. "This stuff could swallow you up."
I bury myself deeper into that rough smell of sun and earth. *Let it.*

When I'm signed back into the ward, I look for Jon to give him the pack of Princetons. The nurse raises her eyebrow. "He's gone."

"What?"

"Yes, he's gone. Bailed out. He's not coming back."

"What do you mean?"

"I'm telling you he couldn't handle it and he's just not coming back."

"But what the hell do you mean?"

"Please, just leave it at that."

And I sit in the TV room, trying to conjure him up to figure out where and how they mean he went. There are so many ways. One night he grabbed the fence and shook it, the whole length trembling.

I remember him telling me about his suicide attempt. The cuts across instead of along the vein, down. "I fucked it up. Did it wrong," he said.

His aunt had told me the same but didn't understand how he'd failed. "Apparently he got it wrong, but I don't see how –"

"He cut across, not down," I say without looking at her but illustrating with a finger running down the length of my arm.

"Oh."

I look up and half-smile, sorry somehow to have told her I know this. "One of those things you wish you didn't know, hey?"

And she looked me up and down and mumured low, "*Ag, my kind*" under her breath. Oh, my child. She could be talking about me or Jon. For a moment I think to myself *but I am no one's child anymore*. No-one's *child*. Lost boy. Lost boy on the far side of the world, and so much sea. There is so much sea.

I have to put my head in my hands to straighten the thoughts again, set them out untangled and coherent.

When I look up again Jon is being walked to his bedroom, nurse at his elbow, and his eyes wide and blank moving over me and down the corridor, where he disappears for the night. Debbie is gone.

Eyes of a dead fish. In the daylight, on land, they are pitiful. Almost ridiculous. Still, you wonder at what they must have seen, wide open as they were, at such depths.

I find the next time group comes round I'm supposed to be in Group 2. The group consists of a middle-aged woman who is practically catatonic, Zintle who is functional and hysterical by turns, Aunty Cee, and now me. We spend our time playing word games with the nurses, who grab the pencil from you and bark out instructions when you get anything wrong. Aunty Cee's been losing since she can't guess English words quick enough. I say, "Why don't you just let her play in Afrikaans?"

They ignore me and dismiss her. "Just play with the rules. No you can't. Just play with the rules." Talking to her like she's inept, or a child. I'm furious.

"Show some respect, damn it. Aunty Cee is the elder here, and you are being unbelievably rude."
"If I'm being rude she can talk to me herself."
"She's too polite for that."
"Just do what I tell you. Your turn to roll the dice."

I rattle the thing as hard as I can. Zintle startles and the catatonic woman moans and puts her head in her arms. I feel terrible and ridiculous all of a sudden, but Aunty Cee's grinning. "You bloody wake them up, my girl."

The nurse looks at me. "Are you angry with me?"

"No, not angry. You haven't yet merited my anger."

"I promise you that if you keep this up I'm going to have you locked in High Care."

"Let's see you try. I'm sure it'll be entertaining."

One of the male nurses walks in and tells me I'm to go with them to the nearby medical hospital. Apparently I'm being sent for a CT scan. "Oh thank GOD. This was unbearable, Carl," I drawl, and saunter out.

They've come to pick me up in an ambulance. "Damn I feel special. Hey, can we put those lights and the siren on, just for a bit?" I ask, all cheeriness and bravado.

The ambulance driver laughs. He's a pleasant-looking young guy. Clean-cut, nervous in the driveway of the psych hospital, wary of me, but not unfriendly.

When we get in, one of them sits in the back with me. I hesitate a moment. "You can sit on that bench there. You don't have to be on the bed."

"Oh thank God. They're always trying to strap you to beds here. Makes you wonder, eh?"

He gives a startled snort of laughter before shooting a

look at the stony-faced nurse, who gets into the passenger seat with the steadiness of a martyr.

I mention how great it is to get away, even for a bit. The driver laughs uneasily, glancing at the nurse. "Ag, it seems like a holiday, eh? Wouldn't mind taking a break there. A nice kind of hotel."
"A hotel where they wake you up at six, medicate you, and tell you what to do all day? Ja. Fun."

He laughs again, softly, embarrassed. I feel bad again, like telling him *I'm sorry I'm being such a sarcastic shit you just don't understand I have to be or they'll eat me alive.* I am holding up so much of the world with that bravado.

The waiting room is packed. About ten patients wait on chairs and in beds. The nurse doesn't leave me for a moment. I idly contemplate the best way to escape. Or I try to, but the truth is I couldn't, even if I tried. I'm not clever enough, and just too damn tired. I'm too tired for the bravado right now. If you had tried to get me to admit it that day I would've spat in your face. I clung to the fact that theoretically I could dodge out the back entrance near the bathroom, but tell myself I can't because the nurse wouldn't let me go to the bathroom unescorted, and that the two ambulance drivers are waiting there anyway. Really I know I just wouldn't know what the fuck to do if I got out.

I settle into the chair. She stands. The room gets steadily hotter. I sit, cross my legs, uncross them, cross them again. Glance at her. It's hot and she's uncomfortable. People, mothers with small children especially, eye me suspiciously. I'm the only one with an escort. If you had asked me then I would've told you how pissed off I was, at the people who stared, at the nurse who never said a word to me, at the whole thing. But really I felt sorry for the nurse, standing while I had to sit down. I was embarrassed at how plain it was that I was under escort, the crazy girl. But I had to stare them down, mock them, lean back in the chair with my legs crossed, roll my eyes at the long wait. And underneath everything I wanted the scans to give me an answer, a name and a cure for everything that had happened.

☼

Doctor's office

At my next appointment with the doctor I hand him a note, folded tight with "FOR GABE" written on it. "Please give that to him. I didn't get to greet him properly, and he was my friend."

The doctor stares at me over his glasses. I've interrupted him in his explanation of the seizure activity found in the scans. "Gabe's a very sick man."

"I don't care. Give it to him please."

"I'll do my best but you know he's a very sick man."

"He's a great man. Please tell me you'll give it to him."

"I'm trying to explain something else right now first –"

"Please just promise me."

" – the seizure activity's been picked up on the EEG."

"Please promise me you'll give it to him."

"He's a very sick man."

And I don't hear much else. I pick it up piecemeal later. For now I stare at the writing pad on his desk, forgetting what I came here for or what the note said or if I signed it properly or what name I'd sign it off with.

⌘

I'm sitting on a friend's dorm room floor, and we're all talking about how shit life can be. I'm not saying anything, I'm choking on spit and anger and this hot, hot thing in my chest. I'm hugging my knees and looking away, grimacing and digging my nails into my wrist when she asks "What's wrong?" I say, "Nothing, love. I'm fine. I'm ok."

She's hanging off her bed, her long hair falling brown and bright, in her pyjamas, and she looks at me and furrows her brow. Like a little kid who's sad for you. "I'm sorry," she says. "I'm sorry you're so sore."
I stare at her, shake my head. "Don't say that. Don't you say that. I'm ok."
"I'm sorry you're so sore."
I look away and blink again and again. "Fuck. Ah, fuck, love."
"I'm sorry for all of it."

And everything breaks, right there. I sob till the tears run out.

The nurse's station

It's Siyanda's last night. He sidles up to me as we queue
for our meds, grins. "Hey, so I'm gonna miss you."
I look at him, try to be nice. "Good luck with stuff."
His face lights up. "Hey! You still haven't answered my
question."
I feel my face fall. "What question."
"Why do some people choose death?"
I stare at him till I'm sure I can speak. "For your sake, I
hope you never find out."

What wasn't said to the doctor

Doctor, things are starting to escape me,
and they'll keep at it you say,
keep running till they're gone,
or washed to blurring, so many words carved and lost
on this ragged slate you map
on scans, point out
patiently. I can control this, stop it with these,
you say. As long as you take them,
it'll curb things.

I'm not afraid of dying, and tonight
I'm going to take a long drag of smoke
and sleep alone. Content
as someone far from any kind of home may be
content, when things follow the course expected.
We take our small comforts this way: maps
and dosages, meds and morning faints,
your voice running over everything
like a loudspeaker, announcing,
interrupting the talking, the loving, the hundred
ungovernable impulses and words, that stupid attempt
at the fence. The night is a front
and my hands are burned.
Tonight I'm going to stretch out on the bed

like a riverbank in moonlight, like a snowbank
in March. Such quiet furies, the rough bones rising
triumphant from the grass.

Sleep easy by your wife
tonight. I mean this with tenderness,
Doctor: it's all I know
how to do, with these my nineteen years
half-caged. Hold
the throat of things, let the blood ring under the skin
in love or violence. Come to know the world
on the edge of a blade singing
with its striving. Take this small quarter
from a tired enemy.

I have never felt the cold
so keenly. My legs
fail me. My hands are too weak
to hold this pen. My name
is a memory
on that rain-marred slate.
But here is the knife-edge I will win it from.
This has hollowed my bones
for flight. Bring them all in, sign
the charts, call it
a difficult night. There's the vial on the shelf,

and my arm so bare
and waiting.

Madwomen have a propensity
for arson, or drowning. Leave nothing
unattended. I am that howl
in the night ward. I am electric
without your help. Rampant. I sing
the nursery songs. It's as they said. Fill the veins
with whatever you've got. Your small life
is beating itself white with fear
as laboratory rats in the half-light. White as the bed,
blank with fear as the bed.

Walks

Every afternoon at 3 we're allowed an escorted walk around the block. Mostly it's the women who go. The women outnumber the men here. Always.

The nurses are winded and shuffle at the end of the line, grumbling, and me and Rowan and Gwen are marching at the head of it, and I yell, "Right ladies, this is it. Split up and serpentine, serpentine!" They laugh, but I'm the only one who tries to make a run for it down a sidestreet. "What the fuck, dude, get back here. *You promised.*" And I scowl and yank a bunch of hibiscus from someone's tree and give it to them, my dears, on bended knee.

When we start walking again Gwen hands out the smokes and her light goes out as some arsehole speeds past yelling "Hey bitches, I like 'em crazy!" and some schoolboys walking home laugh and suddenly our white bracelets feel very bright. So I say fuck it and take out my phone and blast Amy Winehouse, and the three of us, we march down the street, belting out "Rehab", giving the finger to every passing car, bright, bright, with hibiscus in our hair and no more fucks to give.

⌘

Months after my last conversation with her, I'm on the phone with my doctor back in Johannesburg. I ask about the baby, the house. She confirms they're both fine. I fight my way, ham-handed into the question – *so, about what we talked about - what about that?*

And now she seems so ready: "Look, we can fight this. Ja we can. It's not going to be as bad as all that, I've been thinking –"
"Yes?"
"You're very strong, and we can get through this together. You can fight this, man."
"What am I fighting?"
"All of this. You can do it."
"And has there been damage?"
"Well you have a neurologist's appointment for the 10th, let's see how that goes."
"You said there was damage last time. But this new doctor says the scan was clear. But did she see the scans?"
"I don't know."
"Alright. Well let's see what the neurologist says, but what's going on with this? How bad are things?"
"Ag, they're not bad."
"Alright. Then what about what you said in our

conversation?"

"Look, I've been thinking, and you're very strong. You can get through this."

I want to throw the phone against the wall. I think I mutter in a fevered rush into the receiver *Can someone just tell me the stakes. Can you give me that dignity. You're saying I should fight but no one tells me what I'm fighting. Don't degrade me. For fuck's sake I've been degraded already. Give me the dignity of knowing what my enemy is. Don't lie. Stop lying. Say it as it is. Say what needs to be said.*

There's a pause, and she says "So, ja. If you fight it. Look, we're adjusting the meds according to when you feel another seizure coming on. So – raise it when you feel you need it. Maybe by 50mg or so, depending. Then we'll see. You're strong, you can fight this. That's my prognosis."

I stare into the late afternoon light, say thank you. Great. Ask about the baby, ask about the house. Hang up.

⌘

The summer I was twelve. I remember salt in my hair. Clothes always half-dry. A hundred white scratches from the tall grass and the rocks.

The moon would rise outside my window and flood the bed, where I slept naked.

Smell of fish blood on my hands. Smell of fynbos and my sweat like dried seawater. Smell of rain and flowers thick in the woods. I bought a jar of Outeniqua honey at a market and ate it over three months using only my fingers. I was drunk on my young life rising in me like a frenzy. In all the dark water, the dream of my growing up, I came up for air that summer and the world was dazzling me.

In old tapestries and paintings, there is a figure known as the woodwose, the wild man. The etymology of the term is unclear. The first part seems straightforward enough, coming from *wudu*, 'wood,' 'forest.'
Our ritual cleansing before prayer is also pronounced *wudu*.

The second part is thought to be rooted in the verb *wesan*, *wosan* 'to be,' 'to be alive.'

I wandered the beaches for hours every day, talking to the voices I heard, and they rose up in me like howls. They were more perfect than any words I've found.

The figure in those old paintings is not unlike the fauns and satyrs of legend, except with a more human form. A wild man.

The voices would tell me things I can't name anymore. I've lost the names for them, but they were the landmarks of my world then. Moonrise, tide, bird-shadow, wind, pain, cold, heat, all of them predicted and marked perfectly by those voices that told me about those things, and more. I looked for a way to keep them, but back then it didn't even occur to me that I should write anything down. They lived in me. Why write down your own breathing?

On the old tarot decks, from Italy and then France, the card known as 'The Fool' is called 'Il Matto' or 'Le Mat.' The card depicts a bedraggled wanderer beset by a dog or a cat, who tears at his trousers. In some older Italian decks the man seems half-faun, clothed in leaves. The archaic term means 'the madman' or 'the beggar.'

The card signifies the spirit in search of adventure – childlike wonder and impulsiveness tied with wisdom gained through folly. The vagabond, a fixture in the imagination and our social life, yet fundamentally removed from society. He teaches through absurdity, through madness.

A man who tortured me loved Joseph Heller. He would say again and again, in clipped and lovely language, how does anyone remain sane in an insane world?

Until the Enlightenment, the mad were seen as wanderers, both of mind and body. Sometimes they were adopted into village life with compassion and charity, sometimes they were imprisoned, ridiculed, or tortured with exorcism or confinement.

Once I dodged the nurses, tricked every one of them on duty into thinking the other had given me permission to go over to Clinical. I pulled up a chair at a table of women and talked and laughed. Then they asked where Zintle had gone and I said away, away. I tried to put into words the scream of it, the wail, moan, what would anyone call it so it could be understood? I don't know what I was saying but one small woman with white hands spoke from the corner – please write this, she said. Please write it. And I nodded and said yes, ma'am, I will.

The modern echo of this card in ordinary playing card decks is The Joker. We use the term 'joker's wild' to signify an unpredictable move, the opportunity to turn the game on its head.

Through his jokes and trickery he held up a mirror to the society that held him both prisoner and at arm's length.

With the Enlightenment came the need to cast off the old shackles of superstition. A secular world governed by man's reason was the new vision for the future. Belief in the unseen, so central to the old religions, was now outdated. Through scientific inquiry, the mysteries of the world would be brought to light and made plain. All things of heaven and earth could be defined, claimed.

I wanted to tell it as straight as I could. I said I'm going to kill them, dismantle the whole broad hurt of it with facts, with truth. My friend looked up slowly from my notes and said no story is ever true. I said it has to be, it has to. There must be one way to tell it. To speak.

The first psychiatric institutions were designed to confine and remove undesirables from the rest of society. This had started around the 15th century, and now, in addition to removing undesirables, those unable to function in a rational society, the hospitals provided doctors with a space and ample subjects for examining the workings of the mind.

How do you claim to be sane if you do not know what insane is? How do you claim reason if you cannot say what unreason is?

I have been told by many doctors that part of the healing process is the move to define and name your illness.

As he was being taken away for confinement in Bethlem Hospital, later to be known as Bedlam, the seventeenth-century writer Nathaniel Lee said, "They called me mad, and I called them mad, and damn them, they outvoted me."

When I was very little I would name my shadow. I thought of it as a brown dog, who loved and followed me everywhere, would protect me. I would hold it in my lap and say it's all right, it's all right you weren't there when it happened. I forgive you.

The *Diagnostic and Statistical Manual of Mental Disorders* (DSM) is known widely as 'the bible of psychiatry.' It provides guidelines and categories for psychiatrists to give diagnoses. When it was first published in 1952 by the American Psychiatric Association, the manual contained

105 distinct diagnoses. The second edition, in 1968, contained 165. In 1980, there were 260. A revision in 1987 added 10 more. The DSM-IV, published in 1994, contains 350 diagnostic categories.

In the mid-1950's, the United States reached a record high of hospitalized psychiatric patients – about 550,000.

Sometimes I walk into an empty room and find myself saying things I don't realize I'm saying till I think back. Like, "Sometimes I could just cry and cry and cry." Saying it just like that. To the fuckin dishcloth.

In December 1950, chemist Paul Charpentier produced the compound chlorpromazine, later marketed as Thorazine. In lab tests the drug was shown to produce indifference to aversive stimuli in rats. The initial search for the compound was propelled by a need to find a drug to produce indifference in surgical patients. An advertisement for Thorazine from the early 1960s shows a huge eye, widened in horror. Under it a bedraggled figure lashes at something invisible, his back to us. Whose eye is that?

It declares: "When the patient lashes out against 'them' – THORAZINE quickly puts an end to his violent outburst."

I have cicadas in my throat. Cicadas at night, bees in the day.

In the decades that followed, the US mental hospital population decreased rapidly and by 1994, the number of hospitalized psychiatric patients was down to 70,000. Thorazine was for a long time credited for this process, known widely as deinstitutionalization, a claim enthusiastically promoted by pharmaceutical companies and psychiatrists. This claim has now been disputed, as during the same period the US government amended its policies and spending on the care of psychiatric inpatients, leading to the dispatch of patients to newly-established community care centers, alleviating the financial burden of caring for patients living in hospitals.

The political and financial factors leading to deinstitutionalization were eclipsed by the more vociferously promoted message that a new 'miracle drug' was responsible for rendering the in-patient care of so many people with psychiatric problems unnecessary.

It sparked the idea that mental health problems could be resolved by chemically altering the brain, that medication could 'cure' psychiatric illnesses.

What the fuck is this, look at us, look at the ones on this side of the glass, we're the healers, for fuck's sake. Look at us, we fucking sing, we laugh, we tell stories. What, Girl, Interrupted? You saw that fuckin movie? What did they do, sing at someone's door? We can top that shit, easy.

It promoted the claim that mental illness was the result of faulty chemistry and electrical signals in the brain, and thus could be dealt with biologically. This gave psychiatrists an element of medical authority and credibility they had always lacked.

So the nurse stands at the door and ums and ahs saying, Cee, have you finished? I need a sample of your – And Aunty Cee's like, For the love of God, you're asking me for my pee, not my life savings. You can have it, sister. You're welcome.

An hour-long session of psychotherapy and investigation into the causes of the patient's illness could be cut to a 15 minute checkup on the progress and side-effects of the medication. Psychiatrists could see more patients in a day.

Pharmaceutical companies quickly realized that in order to keep selling drugs and broadening their market, they would have to produce medications to treat a range of mental disorders. But that could only be done if there were more mental disorders to treat. The DSM, in defining more and more sets of 'symptoms' as indicative of mental disorders, accomplished just that.

The global market for psychiatric pharmaceuticals was estimated at $80 billion in 2010, with an expected compound annual growth rate of 1.9%, to reach a value of $88 billion in 2015.

He had been hospitalized before, and they'd forcibly medicated him. He could feel it coming on again, and knew he'd be admitted again. That's why he did it.

While at first the hoped-for psychiatric 'miracle drug' would have been a cure, now it is the default assumption that most mental illnesses are chronic, requiring lifetime management with drugs. A chemical cure would mean a decrease in psychiatric patients.

It is the goal of scientists all over the world to find 'the cure for AIDS,' to 'cure cancer,' to 'wipe out malaria'. But the symptoms for these illnesses are definite, largely incontrovertible.

Any behaviour considered excessive, extreme or

unsuitable, can be counted as a psychiatric symptom. And I have never seen a campaign to 'wipe out schizophrenia,' or 'cure depression.'

Critics of the DSM often describe its approach as that of 'a Chinese menu'.

And what comfort can I give? Every day my anxious parents and friends asking, "Did you take them? Promise you'll take them."

You realize they don't really help. All they do is dull you enough to not do anything about it.

"Still, promise me."

There is no right to refuse, no credence given to your words. Cancer patients still have the right to refuse chemotherapy.

At a lecture by a pharmacologist on "alternative medicine" I ask the lecturer what he suggests as an alternative for people forced to take psychiatric drugs with harmful side-effects. He says there really isn't anything.

But what about someone whose medication has debilitating

side effects? Don't they have the right to refuse them? To seek "alternative" treatment that doesn't have those effects?

He huffs, mutters, "Yes, but see I knew this woman who lived down the road from us, and she had bipolar. Really badly, and one day she just went manic and was quite impossible. She had to be forcibly medicated which isn't ideal, but really, she was just impossible."

With the doctors who hold a chart with small check marks near each line:
The Seroquel is poison.
"It calms you, though."
I can't move my body or show any facial expression. Inside it's all still agony. All it does is paralyze me.
"It helps you sleep though, doesn't it?"
It makes every part of my body, even my eyelids, heavy. I only fall asleep later, because there's nothing left to do.
"Ah."
Do you know what they call it in clubs and on the street? They call it SuzieQ. Do you know why you can sell it on the street? Because it's a date rape drug.
(after a pause) "I'm so sorry. It must be terrible to take it."
I told you, it's poison. But you're not going to take me off it, are you? Or if you do you're just going to replace it with something else.

"Maybe something with different side-effects. Not that paralysis..."

In the psychiatric journal, *Schizophrenia Monitor*, an article discusses abnormal and absurd behaviour shown by psychotic patients. It mentions the case of a man who had the words "I don't want haloperidol" tattooed on his forearm.

He swings his pink slippers while he sits on the examining table. The doctor hates him. I wish they'd given us a different room to sit in. I wish he'd chosen to sit on the other armchair, but he perches on the examining table, says You gonna tell them? You gonna tell my story? And I say maybe, I'll try. He says good. Thank you. I want to tell. They put me on this shit, they lock me up and they hate me because I was wise to their shit. You and me, we see more. They just see a thing, we feel the thing. We're wise to their shit. Will you tell them? I say I will one day. I'll try.

When I tell a psychiatrist I find value in what happens when I'm off the meds, that I think there's wisdom in it, that it may even be a gift, he looks at me for a long time, says, "Don't glorify it. Don't fall for it."

A friend says, when you finish it, when you finish writing it, telling it, write, "amen".

When I was thirteen, I went to the school psychologist thinking *Now, now I will tell. Now*. I was diagnosed with clinical depression and started on Cypralex.

When people asked the 9th century Daoist poet Han-Shan about wisdom, he would laugh wildly.

⌘

On the 10th, just as my doctor in Johannesburg instructed, we drive to Port Elizabeth. It's one of those brassy days, the sun unrelenting, nothing gentle or patient about it. Our medical aid's exhausted so I count out the cash for the consultation, and the EEG. The nurse says if the doctor deems it necessary there may be more. We wait. After about half an hour a nurse calls me into a consulting room, and they lie me down on a table.

When they turn the lights off for the EEG the technician asks me to breathe deeply. In and out, deep heaving breaths till I'm hyperventilating. My heart's fast as a rabbit, lungs seizing, and he's there again, whispering, pulling at me, and when the strobe lights are turned on I'm not in the room anymore but on a broad brown plain beaten down by sun. There are lambs and goats being slaughtered, and their cries surround me. Everywhere raw meat and blood, wide staring eyes. I don't see the faces of the people slaughtering them, only flashes of hands and knives. Finally a horse, eyes staring and a handspan from my face, standing skinned and still alive, breath heaving. My brother stands beside me, says he can make it go away. He tries to put the bull's skull over my face, the horns curling into a stag's, then sharper again, moving like smoke. I say no. I reach out to touch the flayed body of the horse, blood sharp in my nose and mouth. He says what will you do, with all these flayed ones? I say I don't know, and he grips my throat and slits it.

I wake up as the lights come on, and they usher me back to the waiting room, then to the doctor's. I'm told he's one of the most accomplished neurologists in the country. He's young, serious but pleasant-faced, and announces with a determined sigh that I have no seizure activity whatsoever.

I sit stunned for a moment. "But what about the scans taken at the clinic –"
"Clear."
"But they said – "
"The technician there has given us several problems with misdiagnosis. He's, er, rather trigger-happy with his diagnoses of TLE. We've had several patients come back to us for reassessment."
"Why did he say I have it if I don't?"
"A lot of doctors don't want to seem stupid."
"But they put me on medication for it. They threatened me with sedatives. Being strapped down. Forced onto medication. They told me I had ten more years to live."

"Yes."

"What do I have, then, if it isn't TLE?"

"Truth be told, I've no idea. What was their other diagnosis?"

"Everything from schizoaffective disorder to bipolar disorder."

"Maybe it's one of those. What are you on?"

"Lamictal."

"Well it's supposed to help with that too, so maybe keep taking it."

A pause. "Hey, what do you do?"

"I'm a writer."

"Many writers have this kind of problem. I guess if you were an accountant it would be a bit more of an issue, but given the right treatment and management of what you have, you could use it to your advantage in a creative way."

I'm quiet. He clears his throat. "I'll clear you for epilepsy, which is great because then you can drive and so on. This is very good news."

"But what do I have?"

"Maybe find another doctor and investigate a possible psychiatric cause."

When we get back to Grahamstown I sit on the bed. I laugh and laugh till I retch.

⌘

The day I was sent to hospital, a two year old boy in Sao Paolo, Brazil, was found with 50 needles pushed into his body. Some of them couldn't be removed because they were too close to vital organs. Particularly the ones embedded in his lungs.

There is a forest called Aokigahara, near the slopes of Mount Fuji, in Japan. It is known as the Sea of Trees, and is the site of so many suicides that there are regular search parties sent out in human chains to scour the forest for the dead or the suicidal. Newspapers use words like "harvest" and "yield".

Also on the day I was sent to hospital, I heard that a little girl of nine was found in an abandoned hostel outside of Johannesburg. She had been gang-raped, and her clitoris cut out.

In France in the 8th Century an epileptic woman was forced to drink salt water, to rid her of the 'demons' that possessed her, and then beaten to death.

The first psychiatrists believed madness in women, hysteria, was caused by the womb moving around the body.

Recently a 14-year-old girl in England was found by her 16-year-old sister. She had hanged herself, after being bullied by strangers online for months. Strangers who had anonymously sent her messages saying, "go cut ur self n die", "do us all a favour n kill ur self", "die, die, die".

A high school girl came into the hospital for three nights. She came in on one of the nights I was swaying with fever, sat down heavily shaking my head, laughing so I wouldn't sob. She sat down beside me and asked "So, are there really crazy people here?"

I said *No, love, no. Don't say that. No one here's crazy. Everyone's just sore. Just sore, deep down.*

She sat down and stared at me while I spoke. *Everybody's just sore. The thing is to be kind, to be kind.* I'm swaying, shaking my head, trying to make her understand. Her eyes filled with tears and she smiled, a small, pained thing, and went to lie down on her bed, not saying another word.

In Saigon, on the third floor of the War Memorial Museum, there is a square vat on the floor near one of the displays. In it there are fetuses, deformed by Agent Orange.

At university someone tells me that a student committed suicide in his room, but was only found when the smell filled the dorm room corridor and made his neighbours complain.

Jon crying bitterly as a child would, hearing about a puppy with a chain cutting into its neck.

At dinner my 15-year-old sister tells me that, "In town someone raped a four-month-old baby and her seven-year-old brother."

Tell me the world is a sane thing, if you can with a clean heart.

⌘

Despite the diagnosis the seizures don't stop. The dog barks at me when the auras come. She barks at the empty air in the room where I go to have the seizure. She will not come near me.

Still a puppy, she keeps pissing in corners, leaving shit on the wooden floor, only gradually getting used to going outside. It's an entirely natural thing that I feel overwhelmed by some days. The schedule of feeding, cleaning, walking, keeping her from chewing up the furniture. One morning, stumbling and worn out from three small seizures the night before, I say to her *I'm too tired. Why can't you be good. I'm so tired. I don't want to give you up but I'm not up to looking after myself, never mind you.* She backs away from me. I sit on the floor and cry. She whines. We are two small things, alone in our separate unfairnesses. Later she curls up to lie down by me. This small life with dark liquid eyes. She depends on me, who can barely walk across the room without leaning against a wall or a chair.

Then at dusk she goes wild. Runs around the house, refuses to come when called. Bites me. Growls and barks at me. When I try to call her using all her nicknames and endearments she does not come near me. Whenever she turns to look at me she stops wagging her tail.

That night, two seizures have me howling and thrashing on the floor, unable to stand. She backs away into her crate, watches, wide eyed, from the floor, far from me.

When it passes, and I lie in bed worn out, she comes to me slowly, settles at my feet, and we sleep without a sound.

⌘

I don't trust any of them. I have no faith in their medication, or any of the names they've given it. Every time I swallowed a pill I was torn in two, always looking for the real medicine. There is a line that no doctor or medication or diagnosis has crossed yet. But I'm familiar with crossings, choices no one gave me. I choose the one I write to you from, out of love. That's all. I broke things and people and lives I could have lived. I went looking for the words for that heart dappled in lightning and dark, that was at the raw core of everything, and I found it, and it ripped out my throat.

He is still there, pacing behind the thousand invisible doors and windows. He paces in the hard Michigan winter woods where he waits. The seawater at the Storms River Mouth, where he waits. He wears a skull that is sometimes a Nguni bull's, sometimes a white hart's, and his arms are torn and strong. There are beads and bones round his neck. He sings in a language I can't pronounce anymore. The words roll useless under my tongue, and I stare, lost but resolute. Past where he stands, language ends. The knife-edge of the world. I do not cross that line. I leave half my heart open. I turn toward the steady work of love. I am praying in whatever language will manage it: *Let me split the silk clean in two.*

I have one foot in that next place of my brother. There is
no wholly coming back from it.

I decided this the night I raised the knife
and my love lay beneath me, saying
"Come back. Come back
and stay with me."

I am a veteran in that next place. I stand straight there.
They hang me with flowers, with banners and brass.
It smells of the blood that rested on my tongue like a
blade that night, and since.

When they said I would die by 30, I went to the hills in
Mpumalanga. I stayed in a village that rises from nowhere
at the turn in the long road that leads to the cliff edge,
where the Drakensberg escarpment plunges into what's
sometimes called The Valley of Death. I walked and rode,
the dog's clear dawn bark beside me.

I was a lonely thing, quiet at last in the place where I walk
along the line between the air and the voices, the bones
of the world and the vivid air.

In Kaapsehoop there are standing stones from 75 000 years ago, used to mark the passing of the sun. An early dispatch said,

"No description could convey anything approaching an adequate idea of the difficulties of a journey through this region.

The mountains are so rugged that only the devil could live here."

I have drawn my knife across my chest to claim
where the wound was. I am singing names
into the smoke in the fired nights.

I tried to tell it as straight as I could. I tried to tell them all. I gathered their names and their stories to me, held it to the flayed skin that I realized too late I'd been wearing all my life.

In those hills ghosts walk among the stones and the thunderstorms come galloping over the ridges. The mist rises always. Always there are birds flying invisible, and the craftsmen make swallows out of blue glass. I was grateful for the death sentence the doctors gave me. It meant no more words, no more summons ringing out in hallucinations and fevers, an end neat as the edge of the world, where the sun drops into the sea. I walked through the world saying goodbye with a clean heart. I learned that we are all of us in this dark place where we maim each other, mute.

They stand and do not cross the line, explaining synapses, chemical processes, telling me on the phone, you'll live, you'll live, you'll live under it always. But they change the names and the medication till I am looking for true medicine, for truth ruthless as the bare rock.

In those hills I ran to, the wind canters clean across the boulders. The town was once given up for ghosts overnight, and a herd of 200 horses bred for the mines went feral.

I am worn to my animal bone and blood.
In the fevered nights my love lay naked beneath me and said "Nature too has no morals," when I could not distinguish her beloved body from the baying,
when I could not recognize the knife for what it was, when I thought
I am holding a river
in those first brutal days of spring.

They hollowed my bones for flight. My life moves in me there, urgent as air.

There is language that comes up spare and bright as bone from a break. It stands beneath us like rock in the place where there is nothing else left. It is the language of *nothing more*.

Nothing is redeemed. Nothing is healed. I am not whole. But the wound is named, and it shines.

Printed in the United States
By Bookmasters